Collected Stories

Volume I

David O. Zeus

This Edition 1.0 Published by DOZ
ISBN: 978-0-9955917-2-1

Disclaimer: This is a work of fiction. Names, characters, places and incidents either are the product of the author's imagination or are used fictitiously. Any resemblance to actual persons, living or dead, events or locales is entirely coincidental.

For Gladys, Alf and Peter.

CONTENTS

Foreword

Not much to say here other than this is a small collection of short stories compiled in recent years while Nigel was musing on Beans. The stories are varied and, I hope, playful. There are more to come...

DOZ

The Legend of Muam Tam Say

– Foreword by Harry's Grandson –

My grandfather must have been in his late-eighties when I knew him and, as my grandmother used to say, he was as sharp as a button. Even as a seven year old boy I could see the young man behind those eyes. It was easy to imagine the smart, young, gentleman traveller and soldier, especially when he recounted those stories of adventures from a world soon to be lost forever.

I have memories in faded-colour of the 1970s sitting in a suburban garden on a hot summer's day clutching my glass of barley water transfixed by the stories of a distant and dangerous world. A world that awaited me. A world I have yet to find and I now realise I probably never will. The stories Harry told came from a life lived in all corners of the British Empire including the green mysterious valleys and snow-capped mountains where this story is set. A place and time beyond the reach and influence of so-called 'modern civilization'.

It would be fair to say that Harry introduced me to story-telling and, as I write this foreword, it is exactly one hundred years after the event it describes, so it is timely that the following (edited) extract from Harry's unpublished memoirs should finally see the light of day.

To the undiscerning, Harry had lived the life of an accomplished public servant – an ambassador to Her Majesty's Government and a much loved father and grandfather. In the 5th Fusiliers he saw action (and was decorated) in the Great War. He lived through a second world war, witnessed a Cold War and the dawn of the space and computer ages. But to a select few, myself included, there was something else about him. Something more. He knew secrets. The secrets unknown to governments, scientists, politicians and journalists.

In his later years he would often regale us with stories of his time in the Middle East and Asia including the end of the British empire in India in 1947, but his family noted that there was one story which pre-dated everything else and always seemed to have a particular hold on him. A story, the telling of which, moved him into a world of quiet, even sad, reflection. The story was an encounter with a natural wonder of the world – the Muam Tam Say.

To this day it is a phenomenon that has never been caught on camera or, as far as I understand, been witnessed since Harry last laid eyes upon one in 1914. For this reason it has fallen into the realm of myth, legend, or even, in our unbelieving age, fiction. In a time of mobile technology when everything is caught in full colour on camera phones and satellites and transmitted across continents in seconds through social media it may seem odd that there is something for which there exists no image nor account written by an actual witness. Except this one – Harry's.

To many far more qualified in the ways of the world, Muam Tam Say are indeed fiction, myth, a legend of the mountains and valleys of faraway lands populated by primitive and superstitious peoples. It was (and is) said that the existence of such a 'wonder' is not permitted by the laws of physics, but everyone who met and knew Harry and was privileged to listen to his words does not doubt the truth and veracity of his story and experience. As Harry volunteered, he was a sceptic himself but, flushed and proud with the open mindedness of youth, he seized the opportunity to investigate the truth when the moment presented itself. He used to say that it was this experience that gave him the mindfulness with which he would live for the rest of his years. I do not doubt it for one minute.

These natural wonders had existed in an oral tradition for many centuries and in the ancient world they were indeed revered, but it is my personal belief that we shall not come across their like again. The world has changed not only in terms of technology and society, but also geologically, geographically and, meteorologically. Besides, if the origin of the phenomenon is true, that it was the pooling of the world's wisdom, then I fear the age of the Muam Tam Say has passed.

For this reason, this short account lifted from the memoirs of Harry Thistlewick, my grandfather, nearly thirty years after his death is especially important. As he reached his twilight years his family implored him to write down his memories and stories. The writings had been thought to be lost so it is a small wonder that they were discovered in a long-forgotten trunk. Not only does this account describe the wonder itself, but it gives a glimpse into the life of a young man at the beginning of his life in the twentieth century and before a terrible war seized the world in a vice-like grip.

I hope this story may prove useful to future enthusiasts. Who knows – maybe a young man or woman clutching a copy of Harry's account will stumble upon another Muam Tam Say. Unhappily, I do not think it will be in our lifetime. So, with a short introduction, read on with an open mind.

By way of introduction: The British had long had an interest in Tibet, in part to counter the threat of Russia's expansion into Central Asia – something the Calcutta-based British Government in India feared. A Tibet under the sphere of Russian influence would provide the Russians with a direct route to British India. Therefore, a British Expedition to Tibet led by Colonel Francis Younghusband, after much bloodshed, reached Tibet's capital, Lhasa, in 1904 leading to the signing of the Great Britain and Tibet Convention after which another treaty between Britain and China was signed in 1906 before the Chinese finally sent a military expedition to establish an administration of the country between 1910-12. However, the fall of the Qing dynasty shortly afterwards resulted in all Chinese forces being expelled from Tibet in 1912 after which the country announced its independence. By 1913 the relationship between Tibet and China was strained to such an extent that the British Government was acting as mediator. This led to the conference in Simla (North India) at which the borders and administration of Tibet were discussed with representatives ('plenipotentiaries') from the British Empire (led by Sir Henry McMahon), Tibet and the Republic of China in attendance.

It was in this context that Grandfather Harry found himself bound for Asia at a time when there were two ways a young man could see the world – as a diplomat or as a soldier (at the time, not mutually exclusive). At the start of his army career Harry was dispatched to British India to familiarise himself with the region. However, on arriving in Simla in Spring 1914 he received instructions to return to London once the Accord was signed for matters in Europe were becoming a priority. The Simla Accord was signed on 3 July 1914 between Tibet and Britain (China having withdrawn from proceedings). Having made an impression on the Tibetan plenipotentiary Lochen Shatra, Harry was invited to return to Britain via Lhasa which Harry reached in the third week of July. Believing he might not have a chance to return to the region, he seized the opportunity to explore as much as he could. If it had not been for the snap decision while preparing for an excursion from Lhasa (as described below) we would not have this one and only written eyewitness account of an encounter with the Muam Tam Say, and for that we should be eternally grateful.

Harry's Grandson

The Muam Tam Say, by Harry Thistlewick (extract from his memoirs)

– I –

When one reflects on four score years lived, small events sometimes lift their heads from the haze of memory to smile and nod at the old man jotting down notes for the succeeding generations (no doubt to ignore). Such events often present themselves as ignominious occurrences at the time of their happening, but take on a weight far greater as time makes its weary way towards ever-encroaching 'modernity'. This is not one of those events. In fact, the event I describe in these passages has never sunk into a haze of memory only to resurface in quieter times. No, this event was life-defining while it happened and is as fresh in my mind as the freshest daisy ever to rest on the bosom of the fairest of maidens. Although only twelve hours in the making, I knew that the afternoon and night I would spend in that Tibetan valley would live with me to my age now, as a frail old man sitting quietly in this leafy English garden.

So, here I write and I hope someone somewhere will read this and take note. God knows my family has been wanting me to put pen to paper. Of all my experiences this is the one that I feel duty-bound to write. I was a witness. If you are a twelve year old boy fascinated my trains, cars and new-fangled gadgets, then you will probably pay attention, but I suspect that if you are a little crusty, you will dismiss this story. If so, please do me the honour and put this book down. What I write is the truth.

In my youth I had the good fortune of having the opportunity to explore the world at a time when travel was rare and a privilege and when I had the vigour, enthusiasm and openness of a young man in his prime. I travelled to places requiring a voyage of many weeks, reaching places where people spoke in wholly unrecognisable tongues. A time before recorded sound and moving pictures. It was also a world before the Great War. The War to end all wars which saw such terrible, terrible suffering and brought Man to the edge of despair – wars have a great way of making the world seem small. Of this story I have no proof, only memories and these words.

It is the story of the Muam Tam Say or the 'Shimmering Sea of Silver Souls'. For some it is folkore, for others a very peculiar, natural occurrence that, some believe, will never be witnessed again as a result of a changing physical environment – plate movements, magnetic fields, orbital shifts or other. But for me, it is real and true and, as the years slip by, as special a moment as I have ever had the privilege to experience. I have never written about it before and I rarely speak of it as my words are usually met with either an incredulity or, dare I say, a polite indifference. And so, without further ado, I'll begin.

Having been sent down from Oxford I often found myself in discourse with my contemporaries about our plans for our futures. Young men bristling with ideas and enthusiasm, they spoke of starting careers, mostly in London, then perhaps finding a nice girl, marrying and starting families and making fortunes. Certainly noble undertakings, but each sounded too onerous to a young man such as myself on the brink of an education in the ways of the world. I would nod and smile as conversation carried on around me, but inwardly I felt bewildered at the absence of their curiosity. A world that lay beyond London's fog and beyond England's shores. I did not see myself as an explorer, far from it, the whole world appeared to have already been charted by intrepid mustachioed men with access to funds too great for a man of modest means. No, I saw myself as a witness. Not on behalf of any fine British institution but for myself, my friends and for those generations to follow. Thus, I looked for a life that would allow me to travel. I joined the army.

As a young man passing out from Sandhurst I was still ignorant of how a life could be hung on small coincidences. As a young soldier with an interest in the politics and the British sphere of influence rather than soldiering itself, I found myself at various briefings and soirees in Whitehall in 1912 and 1913. It was at one such soiree for the Indian Staff Corps that I met Sir Arthur Henry MacMahon and my life took a most welcome direction.

In 1912 China's Qing Dynasty had fallen and the Chinese forces had been expelled from Tibet's capital Lhasa. Although acting as intermediary between Tibet and China, the British were motivated by their interest in keeping the borders secure and keeping the Russians at bay. A conference at Simla (in British India) was convened to discuss Tibet's status and boundaries. Sir Henry who was himself born in Simla and a Lieutenant Colonel in the Corps had been appointed as the British representative at the conference. Learning of my interest in mountaineering and, dare I say, impressed by my albeit primitive understanding of the politics of the Central and East Asia, he suggested I visited him in Simla for a conference with the Tibetans and the Chinese Government.

Before the evening was concluded Sir Henry had offered to submit a formal request that I attend the conference on the grounds that a military observer would be advantageous to the Foreign Office. The request was granted and I was given leave to travel to Simla to learn about the region firsthand. I privately took delight in thinking I would be within striking distance of the Himalayas.

Some of my soldiering contemporaries were envious of my posting, others indifferent, preferring the rounds of parties that London had to offer; parties of which I had soon grown tired. In 1914 I left a cold, damp London and headed to India. Maybe I was just young and impressionable, but the sheer size of Asia was difficult to comprehend for a twenty-four year old young man brought up in the Home Counties. Having spent three years in Oxford I regret to say, I felt somewhat smug of my erudition, but reaching Asia the whole landscape seemed to take on a mantle of a much older wisdom. The wisdom of ancients.

– II –

My business in Simla concluded, I headed north through Nepal towards the great mountains. Everything about the geography of Tibet – derived from the Arabic and Turkic words for 'The Heights' – was immense. Not only the mountains themselves but the Tibetan plateau (the size of western Europe and the main source of water for Asia). It is these vast expanses which give an intimacy to the settlements.

My travelling itinerary had long been dispensed with and I was now exploring the world as God intended – without expectation, without demands and with a sense of humble appreciation. Wherever I went I looked for clues to the sites of interest that were held dear by the local people for reasons long forgotten. Places around which communities and stories had been built. As I headed to Lhasa I picked up a travelling companion, a dashing young man of my own age called Edgar Fitzpiers. We were loading up our mules in a dusty corner of a small settlement in the shadows of the great mountains enjoying our trek from the capital into the valleys when our guide was approached by one of his cousins. Taking a few steps away from us they spoke quietly to each other, initially I assumed the subject of their discussion was about the arrangements for our return to Lhasa. Being a linguist I strained my ears in the attempt to follow their meaning. My assumption had been misplaced. The topic of their conversation was entirely different, but I still had trouble following the meaning, but it was when those fateful whispered words fell from the cousin's lips that the jolt to my senses did occur. Its origins were not from my days at Oxford, my briefing at the Foreign Office or training at Sandhurst, but, I soon realised, my days at boarding school in Yorkshire.

I had a distant memory of reading about Muam Tam Say as a boy, perhaps tucked up at night under the bed sheets at school with a flashlight. Now I cannot be sure. Too many seasons have passed and my memory is unclear. At times I catch myself wondering whether it was one of those happy imagined memories. A flight of fancy in reverse if you like. I've looked for the book and although I have come across other books which describe ancient mysteries of long-forgotten phenomena, none of them mention 'the legend' about which our Tibetan guides were speaking. Yet, as I grow older, I am convinced that I did read about it somewhere. I must have done for why else would I immediately react to the words 'Muam Tam Say' as whispered by that man, our guide's cousin, near Lhasa ten years later? Amongst different peoples it is known by other names (such as 'Jhilamilata Prana Samudrama' and 'Linghun Yin Hai').

The three words stood out of the babble of talk like a clashing cymbal on a cold Spring morning. Before the last syllable of the phrase had melted into the chill of the

Himalayan air I had stopped buckling the mule and turned to our guide.

'Muam Tam Say?' I asked, suddenly alive with curiosity. Both men looked at me with the sharpness of a kukri, and there we stood, the three of us locked into a three-way gaze with only the sound of the restless mule behind us. 'Muam Tam Say?' I repeated. 'Jaham? Nali? Where?'

Their eyes did not fall from mine lest it feed my curiosity. Still no response. I reached into my pocket and pulled out my brown leather wallet. I turned it over in my fingers. The point made, the cousins retired to converse quietly. I learned later that a request to visit a Muam Tam Say could not be refused. It was believed that the Shimmering Sea of Silver Souls belonged to the whole world and therefore no descendant of a departed soul could be turned away if they wished to pay their respects.

'Muam Tam Tim Said what?' said Edgar appearing at my side suddenly alert to the tension in the air. I did not respond, focusing all my attention on our guides. After a few curt words, my guide turned to us and nodded. I made to open my wallet, but he waved a finger.

'Muam Tam Tom Said what?' asked Edgar again somewhat irritated.

'Change of plan,' I replied turning to him, 'slight detour.'

'Why?' he exclaimed.

'Three days?' I said to the guide holding up three fingers. The guide shook his head and held up eight stubby, strong fingers.

'You get five extra days at least,' I said to Edgar who was not warming to the idea. The original plan had included three further days of hiking before returning to Lhasa.

'So, what is it?' he called after me no doubt sensing my determination on sticking with the new plan. I turned and smiled and tried to give him a reassuring nod, but he was not happy. Truth be told, I was not sure myself. I only had a memory of reading about it as a boy. The Shimmering Sea of Silver Souls. The place where all men's souls gather on their way to the next world. The irony is that in his subsequent retelling of the encounter, Edgar was more enthusiastic about it than I ever was. More enthusiastic about a trip that almost never happened.

I met Edgar once or twice at gatherings both informal and formal in England the following year. The evening would not conclude until he had related the encounter with a rare natural wonder in the Himalayas to a rapt audience of wide-eyed young women and disbelieving, but nonetheless captivated, envious men. He would turn to me and try to include me in the story-telling but, as the eyes fell on me, I felt the desire to share ebb away. It was an experience too personal, too noble to debase with words over canapés or port. Had he lived I have no doubt he would have continued to tell the story to anyone who would listen. Sadly, Edgar's first-hand recollections to enrapt families and friends would not last beyond the war. He was killed two years later. I carry the sadness of his loss with me to this day. Not only the loss of a good friend, but also the loss of an accidental travelling companion who was with me the day I laid eyes on the Shimmering Sea. For a man never short of a word or reaction, his response to the sight across the valley was no different to mine – wordless, breathless awe. It was almost as if the sight of the Sea of Souls drew a part of one's own soul towards it, a glimpse of the place we should one day reach yet from which we would never return.

The stories of the Shimmering Sea and its origins and meanings varied, no doubt corrupted in translation, embellished and romanticized in a re-telling and possibly falsified for illicit gain and attention. In centuries past Westerners had also tried to account for the phenomenon and to this day I don't believe science has adequately explained its existence. Theories abound, but none authoritative. Perhaps the scientific instruments of today could explain how it occurred, but until it returns, humanity will never know. Perhaps that is how it should be.

My inadequate research suggests there exists no written 'witness' account of the sea. There are references to its occurrence extending back to before Tibetan Buddhist teachings and Mongolian and South Asian folklore passed down by word of mouth through generations. The phenomenon is only to be found deep in rural areas and the respect shown to the community's dead meant news of an occurrence did not travel far. Believing the soul to be the host, the seat of a person's wisdom, the sea was thought to be home of the accumulated wisdom of the world. As the sea grew, so did the wisdom of mankind. As people passed away, their souls had one last duty – to join other departed souls in the Sea of Silver Souls. It was accepted that the sea would eventually collapse and the wisdom of the long-departed would be washed away. Its collapse was not through the fragility of the sea itself, but forced by the increasing folly of men. Following a collapse of a Muam Tam Say, it was said that the world would be plagued by wars and pestilence. Another sea could only rise when the souls of men carried sufficient wisdom to their death. A wisdom borne of peace.

Although no person who wished to visit the sea could be turned away, its guardians who knew the location of the sea were loathe to publicise it, not only because the priests and the local people wished for solitude, but they held the sea and all it represented in great esteem. It was feared that not only would a scene of tranquility be corrupted by the gaze of travellers, but interference might precipitate a collapse of the sea itself. Even though wars and pestilence might not directly find their way to the foothills of the Himalayas, Tibet, as the home of wisdom, had a responsibility to the world. Besides, the pragmatists felt that unrest in the world would have an affect on the provinces, trade and local politics. Before the twentieth century the written and spoken word travelled at the walking pace of man or mule, so news of an occurrence of the sea would seldom reach far beyond the mountains and valleys. By the time interested outsiders had tracked down its supposed location, the visitors (be they scientists, historians, philosophers, explorers) would be met by a dirty patch of soil, shrub and mud. Thus Muam Tam Say remained largely unknown, existing quietly on the valley sides before disappearing only to reappear decades or centuries later. It was myth and legend to all but the lucky few.

– III –

I was blessed to become one of the lucky few on a late afternoon in late July 1914. To this day I do not know where we were. As Edgar and I followed our guide, one valley turned into another and day moved into night and back into day. I asked the guide 'Yarlung River?' but was met with a frosty glare and a shake of the head. The Yarlung had cut its way through the Himalayas forming the steepest, deepest gorge in the world. Travelling first on rough tracks then through forest, we were to all intents and purposes lost. I cannot be sure for how many days we travelled. The weather was temperate and the heat of the sun tamed by the canopy of trees. The views, of course, were spectacular. There is something about that part of the world which re-orders a man's heart, soothes his ambitions and lessens the inclination to withhold. Edgar's frustration at the slightest change of plan had melted into a warm embrace of nature as we made our way down valleys, up inclines into lush vegetation and past barren rocky outcrops, across rope bridges and deeper and deeper into the green valleys overseen by the kindly gaze of the snow-capped mountains rising high in the distance.

One late afternoon we guided the mules along a rocky path shrouded on the valley side by eucalyptus trees running the length of the valley. Adrift in a world of my own with just the occasional observation from my travelling companion and the smacking of the mules' hooves on the path I became aware of our lead guide slowing to a stop. I looked up and saw him raise an arm and point through the veil of greenery to the other side of the valley.

I followed his gaze through the leaves, my eye scanning the valley side two, perhaps three, miles away looking for the prize. Having never seen an illustration of the wonder, I was unsure about what to expect. I saw a mountainside covered in trees and fauna and beyond that the majestic backdrop of snow-capped mountains. Nothing looked different from the vistas of the previous days. The trees were broken by grey rocky outcrops and rock falls, hidden by wispy clouds being stretched and pulled up and over the tops of valleys and mountains or twisting and swirling down the valley sides. It was a few seconds before my eye fell upon a view so very few people have seen. It wasn't a grey rocky break obscured by cloud, but a silver and grey structure in which hints of the surrounding lush greens were reflected. The object shimmered slightly in the low afternoon sun. Focusing my gaze I could see what I understood to be indeed the rippling of its surface – water.

'Muam Tam Say', the guide said. 'Muam Tam Say.'

'What is it?' asked Edgar coming to a stop behind me.

I said nothing. Still transfixed by the image across the valley, my mind was trying to make sense of what I was seeing.

'Muam Tam Say,' said the guide for the final time.

I sensed Edgar turn and look across the valley himself.

Mute, I stood transfixed. Together two young Englishmen looked in silence at a sight that would stay for us for our lifetimes – the first view of the mythical lake. The Shimmering Sea of Silver Souls, Muam Tam Say.

What is so special about this sea? Well, a sea is flat and sinks into the earth and, to the earthbound observer, looks like a mirror lying flat on the ground. But this was not so with the Muam Tam Say. It is no flat, land-hugging lake. It is inverted. The flatness is on its underside and its watery depths rise into the air in an almost perfect half-sphere. Like a drop of water it sits alone and proud on the earth's surface rising above the trees and rocky surroundings. The blue of the sky, the green of the land reflected in its shimmering silverness almost camouflaging itself. Even from several miles distance across the valley, one could make an estimation of its size by comparing it to the surrounding trees and tiny figures moving around its base.

'It must be over one hundred feet high,' gasped Edgar.

I tried to nod in agreement, but had slipped into a stillness all of my own. The only discernible movement was my slight breathing and a rising of my eyebrows in acknowledgment.

'And what, over two hundred feet across?' he continued shaking his head in disbelief.

We followed the rocky path down to the floor of the valley, across a rope bridge and slowly up the incline on the other side largely clear of vegetation. Our gaze never left the spectacle. As I approached I endeavoured to find words to articulate my wonderment for I knew that there would be a time when I would recount this moment to my children and, by God's grace, to my children's children, but the language of Shakespeare failed the challenge. It was no surprise that there were no written witness accounts of Muam Tam Say. I felt like a traveller from the age of the Pharoahs reaching the Nile and seeing the three gleaming pyramids each clad in marble and topped in gold.

In our times, rarely do we see a sight for which we are not prepared. A sight that truly imbues in the viewer a sense of marvel in the world. As we made our way across the valley, one could discern the flow and eddy within the structure itself. The sea, for that is the only way to describe it, had a soothing, penetrating calmness. The valley's breeze moved invisibly around the valley, swirling around the trees, tripped up by outcrops of rock, but as it passed over the sea and caressed its surface, the breeze carried the water's coolness with it, refreshing its admirers further down the valley. A cool balm for travellers' weary spirits.

– IV –

As we neared the sea, we could see that its base was surrounded by a fence of blankets, shawls, rugs hanging from rickety posts and swinging gently in the wind, which reminded me, somewhat ungraciously I confess, of old neglected tennis court nets at my old school during winter. Human figures moved slowly back and forth along the fence reinforcing the grandeur and scale of the structure dwarfing and dominating them.

We would use any excuse – adjusting the luggage on our animals, checking the security of our footing – to slow, pause and drink in the sight before us. The sea did not demand our immediate presence, it invited us to join it at our leisure. I believe I have never moved so slowly as I did that afternoon. It took us a full two hours to make our way across the valley floor and not a word was spoken. We knew that we would approach the sea for the first time only once in our lives.

Alas, good things come to an end and our approach concluded with a small climb up a limestone path to the valley side fifty yards to the west side of the sea. Our guide tied our trusty animals to stakes driven into the ground in a small grazing area and waved to a boy to bring the mules some water. I watched the creatures start to feed themselves on the tough grass and was just as amazed that they seemed wholly unimpressed by the spectacle beside them. Did they know something we didn't? Were we the only creatures in God's kingdom able to appreciate such a wonder? How could any living thing not marvel at the sight on this side of the valley?

Edgar and I walked slowly towards the sea that rose high above us and observed what I assumed were priests and locals strolling along the immaculately maintained footpath running the circumference of the sea. A handful of old men and women sat at intervals along the path shaded from the late afternoon sun by the hanging drapes and rugs. Almost the height of a local man, the woven cloth wall looked tired and was the only clue to the 'age' of the sea and the time it had been accumulating souls. One could just discern the route of previous paths that the sea had now claimed. When had holy men tread those now-submerged paths – forty, sixty, one hundred years earlier?

I was unsure about the protocol of visiting the site. I turned back to our guide who was locked in a discussion with a holy man; no doubt catching up on the local news. Seeing my indecision, the guide waved me towards the sea. Touching Edgar's elbow I took the first of two dozen steps towards the shimmering mountain of water. Edgar's eyes hadn't moved from the object. He had hardly uttered a word for two hours. (A legendary occurrence in itself.)

We stood side by side in front of this curved wall of water watching the gently swirling patterns within. It looked 'deep'.

Of course it was, it was over two hundred feet across. I could not discern any structure or shape within the sea that might somehow support the shape thus allowing a scientific reasoning for its existence. It was indeed like a giant raindrop that had fallen to earth. Edgar reached out and touched the surface running his fingers across the sea. It behaved as you might expect any normal body of water. Droplets ran over his fingers and dripped off his hand into the sand below.

Suddenly nervous that he had somehow perpetrated some vile act on the sacred object, we turned around. I understood Edgar's instinct to touch, but I felt a pang of nervousness in case the human touch would break the magical seal making the sea collapse into nothingness in a few violent seconds. We saw an old man sitting on a blanket off to the side watching us; a warm smile buried in his weathered features, evidence of a life lived outdoors. He was surrounded by small cedarwood bowls. He picked up one in each hand and offered them to me and Edgar. I approached him slowly and nodded thanks as I took the proffered bowl. As I did so, I caught sight of another man a dozen steps away who, clasping a similar bowl in both hands, gently scooped water from the Muam Tam Say, muttering a few words under his breath as he did so. After uttering what I took to be a prayer he tipped the water over his head. Now satisfied that I was not going to cause any great offence, I returned to the sea's side and grasping the small wooden bowl in both hands gently scooped out a bowl of shimmering water. It came away from its parent with ease. Sitting in my bowl the water was flat. There was no indication the water was holding a shape that was untoward.

Like the holy man I had just seen, I lifted the bowl up and offered a few words of thanks to the millions of departed souls who had brought me to this place of wonder. Tilting my head forward, I poured the bowl's contents over the back of my head. The coolness slapped the neck and ran quickly under my collar and down the spine cooling and refreshing the whole of my body and bathing me in a serenity borne of nature and far away from the heat and angst of men flustered by ambition in a forever busy world.

I left Edgar and walked around the circumference of the sea. It was a cathedral to one of life's four elements. I passed a few holy men, a handful of travellers and a few locals. No words were exchanged, just nods of acknowledgement. It reminded me of my ventures into the monastery adjoining my school in Yorkshire; people affected deeply on a personal level but brought together in a quiet community of contemplation of something greater and unexplained. Something all the greater by its quiet understated revelation to Man.

I passed old men raking the gravel path, others mending the fence of rugs. The path ran around the rear of the sea, but was overhung with vegetation and trees on the valley side. A branch from one such over-hanging tree hung low and close to the surface of the sea. As the gentle breeze swept along the valley side the tree swayed, the leaves of the branch dipped in and out of the Muam Tam Say kissing the surface like a nervous first love. I must have stood and watched this dance for a full ten minutes. Part of me wanted to pull the branch down and break off a leaf to take away with me as a reminder to myself not only of the sea itself but how we should witness even the simplest of life's daily wonders. The other part of me felt that it was not my place to disturb anything. The witness to the event should be my eyes and heart alone and not the selfish possession of another, for that is what we all were – leaves, vegetation, the lush valley itself – we were each present as witnesses.

Returning to the southern aspect of the sea I noticed a handful of small channels dug across the gravel path under the rug-fence leading into an open space in front of the sea and down into the valley. With some disappointment I realised that those tending the sea were preparing for the souls to fulfill their destiny and pass through to the other world. All Muam Tam Say collapse eventually and the preparation for the inevitable dispersal of water was only proper, but I would be misleading any reader if I did not confess that this sight filled me with sadness, even dread.

My legs tired, I turned away from the Muam Tam Say and stood looking over the fence down across the valley. Ever mindful of the vast presence behind me, I breathed slowly. My world was silent but for the gentle lapping sounds of the rippling water behind me. I felt a touch on my arm and turned to see Edgar. He nodded to the east side of the sea. I followed him to find yet another old man warming some tea over a small fire.

– V –

Refreshed in mind, body and spirit by the tea, I slipped away from Edgar and the priests into the valley below and found a quiet place on the grass two hundred yards from the water. My breathing slowed as I lay flat and looked up at the clouds melting and turning in on themselves in the otherwise sharp blue sky above. The sun was no longer reaching the valley, but its light still bathed the mountain tops in colour and warmth above me. As I closed my eyes I imagined these huge mountains to be the prehistoric guards to the Muam Tam Say.

I watched the clouds – huge mountains of sunlit white craggy cliffs rolling over and over only to crash down into the troughs of grey shadow. From the silence of the valley side, I marvelled at the grace of the drama taking places miles above me as I lay flat in the cool green valley. These huge mountain ranges of cloud, dwarfing their earth-bound Himalayan cousins below, were built then torn apart before my eyes. The result of hundreds of millions of years of geological forces, the Himalayas had inspired and challenged men, but their massive cousins above them were barely acknowledged, their own power and majesty ignored.

I watched as one bulkhead, a craggy outcrop the size of four mountains slowly built up and began to roll and arch up above a valley of shadow. Its awesome, rounded peak soon reached beyond the support of its mountainsides. Within minutes the white mass had collapsed and swirled down into the white ravine below – lost forever and never to be remembered bar for these few lines.

As I dozed I wondered what it would be like to scale those ethereal mountains. To climb an ever-moving mountain, to journey across a brilliant white landscape. And as the cool air slipping off the sea behind me bathed me in serenity, my breathing eased and I slipped into a deep, deep sleep.

And then I was there – in the cloud mountains themselves.

With my crampons and my trusted leather back-pack, I was heaving myself up a steep incline. Much like climbing the 300 foot high sand dunes in the Western Sahara, the cloud underfoot moved yet was just firm enough to hold my weight. Unlike the sand deserts, however, I was moving fast across the ever-changing mountainscape. Or rather the mountainscape was moving fast across the sky. As I took two or three laborious steps, the white mountainside travelled a thousand feet skywards. The peak, which had been ten miles above me, began to fall away out of view as I raced toward it. I paused and gripped the moist white cloud below me. Bereft of any physical form, it melted through my fingers. I glanced down and could see the unmoving, mountain ranges of rock and dust miles below me. A part of me hankered for certainty underfoot, but I knew that the exhilaration of my vantage point should not be missed. Should travellers in the valley below care to look upwards as they made their way along gravel paths, through forests of eucalyptus trees, they would struggle to see the tiny, tiny black dot being tossed about on a white, churning mountain in the sky. A traveller would not hear my cries as I slipped and fell through gaps in the white valley floor to the solid earth below. I would be just another climber of white mountains lost to the earthbound world.

Turning my attention back towards the white mountaintop above me, I watched as I approached it at a terrifying speed. Its peak, repeatedly turning in on itself, was falling beyond into an abyss. The rush of cold air was deafening. Suddenly a rolling, swirling boulder of white began racing down towards me, possibly stirred by the lie of a solid mountain hidden below. It seemed my fate was not to reach the peak, but to be swept off the mountain altogether by a breakaway block of wind and moisture the size of a large house. I gripped the cold air tightly and dug my feet into the soft mountainside and braced for the impact of the tumbling house of cloud. I closed my eyes, breathed out and began to take my last breath when I was hit by an almighty force.

As the raging, swirling block hit me, it ripped every last thought, feeling and experience from me tearing them from my soul, cleansing me of any memory before leaving me, shivering but alive. I opened my eyes and saw my fingers dug deep in the soft white mountainside and my feet sunk up to my ankles in the freezing softness. Thoughts, feelings, experiences feed into our personality, direct our reactions as we age – our wilder inclinations are tamed; our perspective sometimes poisoned – but the tumbling house of cloud had cleared me of such clutter.

I looked down the slope and saw the block rolling away far, far below. I saw no sign of the thoughts, feelings and experiences it had ripped from my being. Perhaps they were wrapped up, crushed, dissolved in the disappearing mass and swirl of white below. As for me, I was pure, clean, re-born. Not only had my aches of body and soul been swept away, but so had my ambitions, plans and hopes. It was an experience of 'nothingness'. Was this enlightenment? It is only when little cracks and crevices appear in the otherwise clean sheen of innocence that the weeds and gravel of life can get hold.

My attention returned to the mountain once more. It had moved and was rolling me up to the summit. Within moments I was there, high over the world, high over two mountain ranges – the immovable snow-topped range many miles below and the cresting, crashing, living, breathing mountain range around me, now a slow-moving, majestic landscape turning and rolling in a serene dance. I imagined myself the creator, an ancient god clicking his fingers and stopping the twisting landscape of cloud, freezing it in that moment. Satisfied with my creation I observed the frozen, white landscape sink earthwards over thousands of years watching as it accumulated dust, dirt and vegetation until it eventually solidified to become the rocky Himalayan range of today. Such was my imagining. Who knows, perhaps we do indeed walk on ancient sky.

My reflections were broken as I realised the summit on which I was standing was again beginning to move rapidly, this time in a downward direction. My gaze fell away from the sun-touched glinting peaks of the horizon to the darkening greys of the trough in front of me. I was on a cliff-top, in fact no, it was a crest of large wave about to break into the shadow below. At first I was unable to discern how far I would fall, but after a few moments it became clear. Horribly so.

I dug my feet into the soft moving features, leaned then sat back into the cloud as it rushed to its own edge and saw what lay beyond the brink. A fall of what must have been four miles, but the trough (or valley) had a weak bottom, for moving directly into sight far below was, what appeared to be, a lake. A deep lake at the bottom of which lay minuscule mountain sides, forests and solid earth. The lake was not a lake at all but a hole in the cloud.

The mountainside fell away vertically. First my hands broke free of the mist on to which they were holding and then my boots were loosened from the security of the hold of the white mountainside. And I fell. Wisps of white passed me as I plummeted earthwards but none were enough to slow my rapid descent, none able to support my weight. I watched as the craggy over-hang from which I had fallen turned in on itself and disappeared. I turned over as I fell and saw the earth far below and the white shimmer of wispy cloud which I had taken to be the surface of the lake. It would be a matter of ten or so seconds before I would pass through and shatter the illusory lake surface on my way to a sudden death. I closed my eyes as I passed through the milky surface of the lake and turned myself over. I'd prefer to end my days facing the sky rather than the dirt. As I prepared to breathe my last I felt a ghostly cool whiteness wrap itself around me giving me a sharp but welcome chill down my spine.

The rush of air through my hair and jacket appeared to slow; its thunder as it passed my ears subsided. I came to a calm and easy rest buffeted by the slightest of breezes. For a moment I thought I had come to stop on a piece of mountainside which had yet to fully solidify since the last god had snapped his fingers, but I opened my eyes to find myself safe on a thick cloud moving swiftly westwards many miles above the hard Himalayas. I watched with relief as the lake through which I had fallen eased westwards at a much slower pace and in the far distance above I could just see the twisted and broken summit from which I had fallen. It seemed so far, far away.

Exhausted, I let my head fall on to a soft white pillow and let the white world carry me to its destination. With my eyes closed, I slumbered, clean, pure and at peace. I don't know how long I was carried forth as the warmth of the sun retreated from the advancing shadows.

– VI –

I began to stir much later. I don't know whether it was the coolness of the moisture of the cloud as it swirled over my head, down my neck and back or the cries of men. I sensed that some were shouting and waving at me from the mountainsides a mile below me. I waved back and closed my eyes again but I was soon shivering and conscious of my wet shirt and hair. The men's cries grew louder. I struggled out of my rest and forced my eyes open. It was dark. Dark and cold. Rising up on my elbows I found myself on the valley side where I had lain the afternoon before. I shivered. My shirt was completely wet, my hands quivering with the cold. Looking down, I saw water streaming over my limbs and down the valley side. As my senses slowly worked up to speed I heard the cries of the men behind me up the incline. Turning I saw men running with flaming torches and waving at each other and at others slumbering on the grass below the Muam Tam Say. Like me, they too were stirring, rubbing their eyes and rising to their feet. Water was pouring down the incline from the sea. The whole valley side was weeping. Was this normal? I rose to my feet and raced up towards where the holy men were guiding the visitors and locals away from the immediate vicinity of the sea.

As I gathered my senses together I became aware of the sound of the water. When we had arrived that afternoon I had been struck by the soothing sound of the sea lapping as its surface rippled. Now, however, and through the din of shouting, one could unmistakably discern the sound of running, babbling water. Was the structure leaking? Did it exist as a result of some sort of membrane holding the lake together; a membrane which had now been punctured? Were the men trying to fix it? I looked back towards the path circumventing the sea and witnessed the holy men racing back and forth ankle-deep in water streaming from the sacred site but doing nothing to fix it. A handful of old men were trying to rescue their belongings from being washed down into the valley. The little channels which I had seen dug across the path were overwhelmed with water and virtually lost to the observer were it not for faster running water seen at intervals along the path.

I suddenly caught sight of our guide racing past me and asked him what was happening. He put his hands and arms together in the shape of a dome and let his hands fall down flat. 'Down,' he said, 'down'.

And then it struck me. Muam Tam Say do not last forever. That is why so few people have seen them and why they are regarded as sacred. They rise up of their own accord over many, many years and then, if circumstances permit, are discovered by shepherds, locals, holy men. By the time word has reached the outside world the seas might no longer exist. And that was what was happening. The Muam Tam Say was collapsing. Its time had come.

The guide raced on and I turned to look at the weeping sea. I heaved a deep sigh of sadness. Sadness at such a wonder being lost to the world. A wonder of the natural world which defied its own physical laws.

Similarly, if a man can rise above the sum of his parts – his physiology, his experiences and prejudices – he can create wonders beyond the laws of his own base nature. But such greatness is rare and fragile.

Although I had only been in the valley for twelve hours I had lost the capacity to contemplate a life beyond the Muam Tam Say. I had stopped. I was reconfiguring my self, my own nature. The Shimmering Sea of Silver Souls is not a place you visit. It is a place you become. The sea reveals itself to you and to walk away and continue one's travels feels unnatural. Perhaps that is why it collapses. Once its wisdom is shared, it must release itself, otherwise why would travellers leave its side? After all, it is the physical manifestation of what all travellers are looking for. Why would they ride on? Amidst the shock and sadness, there was, deep inside me, my own sea of contentment. I had been bathed in its coolness. I had been given this opportunity to witness this wonder of the natural world. I knew I would never lay eyes on such a sight again. My breast rose with elation and pride then sunk with sadness.

Over the next two or three hours the Muam Tam Say continued to weep. A wide-eyed and anxious Edgar had found me. He too had fallen into a deep slumber on the hillside below the sea and had been woken by the shouts and water streaming down over his head and feet into the valley. Now as the sun hung an hour old in the early morning sky, he sat with his head in his hands waiting for the inevitable. At about seven o'clock in the morning all holy men, guides, merchants and visitors were sitting or standing on either side of the wonder as it breathed its last.

A conversation with the guide later revealed that it was quite normal for people to have dreams in the shadow of Muam Tam Say. Dreams were the sharing of the pooled wisdom held within its watery walls.

The sea was now about two-thirds its size the previous evening, perhaps seventy feet high at its apex. The overhanging branches from trees higher up the valley side which had kissed the surface the night before, hung limply in space forty feet from the surface of the sea. As the early morning warmed, my sadness had been replaced by reflection. I was not witnessing a demise, a death, but a release, a re-birth – much like a young man leaving the childhood home to explore the world for himself. It was indeed a time of pride for those of us who had witnessed its infancy and youth.

Soon after seven o'clock that morning, a ripple or wave seemed to pass once, twice, three times though the body of water in quick succession and then the Muam Tay Say collapsed. It must have taken all of five seconds for the sea to fall in on itself pushing large waves ten feet high down the valley side sweeping the wall of blankets away like tissue paper. The sticks to which the blankets had been attached tumbled away like tinder wood. In one almighty whoosh, the sea that had secretly drawn men and women in whispered reverence breathed it last and melted into the landscape. A rush of air affirming its departure.

Edgar, our guides and I stood with the community of witnesses watching the wonder slip away only to be anointed by a fine spray from its sacred waters. A few men who had been sitting further down the hillside were swept away by the waters but were rescued, bruised and cut a few minutes later.

Cleansed from head to foot by the mists and the blast of cold air generated by the collapse, I opened my eyes to a different landscape. Small figures of men and women hundred of yards away began emerging from the trees on the far side of, what had been moments before, the sea.

Making my own way through the trees I entered a clearing several hundred feet across. Uneven, bereft of vegetation, the clearing was strewn with small rocks. Stepping onto the clearing itself, the footprint of the Muam Tam Say, my foot sunk into the soft earth. The last remnants of the sea oozed over my boots. Other than these simple clues to the presence of the sea, no pools of water remained on the site. I walked in silence with dozens of others in quiet circles living the last minutes of the Shimmering Sea of Silver Souls.

– VII –

Edgar and I stayed at the site for the remainder of the day and the following day. Nothing could tear us away. Early on the morning of the fourth day we loaded our mules and joined our guide after breakfast on the path whence we had first come. I took one last moment to walk on the site of the Shimmering Sea. Small green shoots could be seen growing through the silt and the cracks in the rock now laid bare. Walking to the centre of the clearing I came across a small pool which had been fed by a tiny trickle of water from the edge of the clearing further up the valley side.

Ah, I thought to myself, more souls have departed their fleshy temples and were beginning their journey home. Muam Tam Say are said to rarely reappear on the same site, but I indulged my hope that I was witnessing the birth of a new sea.

We travelled onward to a few other valleys and settlements before eventually returning to what was commonly known as 'civilisation', Lhasa fifteen days later. Since that day Edgar and I have carried the memory of the Muam Tam Say with us and although we hardly spoke about it during those fifteen days, the days themselves spoke of nothing else but our experience; a never-ending chatter of silence. At Lhasa we parted ways. Edgar headed south-west to Katmandu, I headed south to Simla before my journey home to England. I have a memory of our final evening together sitting outside a small local establishment drinking tea and talking quietly about the sacred site. Being young, I thought I would have other wondrous experiences, come across other precious marvels of the world, but no, there were none. At that moment I felt my time with the sacred phenomenon was far too fleeting, but as the years have passed I have realised I did indeed have sixty years with it. If treated with care, experiences do not decay.

I have on the rare occasion spoken of my experiences in that place near the Yarlung River, always preferring to reflect alone on those twelve hours. On the other hand, Edgar, on returning to England, was happy to brag. I miss him still and his loss on 1 July 1916 on the first day of the Somme, twenty-three months later, fills me with more sadness as each day passes. Oh, how splendid it would be to sit in my garden and raise a glass and whisper our memories to each other, but it was not to be. I sometimes think, perhaps his soul has found a Muam Tam Say of its own hidden deep in some lush valley. It was not lost on me that the collapse of the sea coincided with the collapse of peace in Europe; a time when wisdom was lost to the world of men.

In stolen moments of peace I reflect on my dream in the shadow of the Muam Tam Say, climbing the mountains of mist and riding the rolling clouds. The images sometimes work their way into my dreams as an old man, but they are images, not the vivid experience of that night. If that Muam Tam Say was indeed the host of ten million souls then I like to think that as I was touched by its water so were the souls sharing their experiences, infusing me with wisdom. A wisdom which challenges man to scale the mountains ahead while soothing him in the fall – all falls, to the wise man, are soft – and a wisdom to know that one should marvel at the view.

– VIII –

Two world wars were to pass before I found myself in north India on a diplomatic mission whereupon I took leave to slip into Tibet. My guide had long since died, but other guides were kind to the old man who enquired after the Muam Tam Say. I managed to convince a few young men who spoke limited English to take me on a trek in search of the once-sacred site. My memory of the location was shaky after nearly thirty-five years and I was not sure I ever found the valley. That is not to say my heart lifted a number of times on descending a path or turning a bend, but I was always to be disappointed. Who knows, perhaps I walked over the very site of the sacred sea, its sandy, solid base now hidden under shrubs and trees and fallen rocks.

I thanked my guides after my trek and bade farewell one late afternoon in August, never to return to those valleys guarded by the high and mighty Himalayas. I noted with sadness when I left my young guides that they, in their broken words, spoke of 'the legend' – the legend of Muam Tam Say and not a Muam Tam Say itself. Two World Wars had made the world smaller and I was a foolish fond old man looking for a mythical place about which he had first read as a boy. But, as I said, I have never come across an eyewitness account of the sea. It might therefore be possible that the young man in this old man was possibly the last witness to a true lost wonder of the world.

Perhaps this short and artless account will find a young man or boy who will commit himself to the quest of finding another Muam Tam Say to bear witness in words. Then, and only then, will it be a legend no more. Should it be you, reader, may God bless you with such good grace in your endeavour. And, please, should you find it, remember me to the

Shimmering Sea of Silver Souls and my dear long lost friend, Edgar. You may even be witness to his watery wisdom. Finally, remember to do one more thing – to lie down and rest nearby. And dream.

The Dot Matrix

– I –

His office day started at nine, but he liked to get there early and have a quiet hour by himself to do all the e-chores of sending emails, paying bills and shopping. Coffee in hand, he stood looking around the empty open-plan office trying to summon the strength for the day ahead. Now thirty-two years of age he had been stuck in that office for six years and it was now proving a challenge. At least the felt-covered, chipboard partitions between the desks put some space between himself and his twenty-something colleagues.

He was at a time of his life when life had no time for him – it had given up and moved on. Or so it felt. It wasn't as if he was lazy or uninspired. He had tried. He had put money and several years into setting up a website business, but the project had failed because people had let him down. The failure of the venture had been an eye-opener and many, many months later he was still feeling beaten up. He had just about cleared his debts thanks to this office job, but try as he may to paddle upstream he would soon find himself swept down the river of despondency.

Although the website project had sunk to the riverbed, a few little pearls of hope were keeping it company. Occasional glimmers of possibility for the project's revival were refracted through the gloom. But did he have the energy? He had been promoted once at work and there were rumours that there might be another promotion in the pipeline. He would be asked for his opinion in meetings. Words would fall out of his mouth, smack the table and dribble across the wood veneer towards his colleagues, some of whom, for some unknown reason, would lean forward and lap them up.

What encouragement he felt from hearing himself speak in the meetings was dissipated by the reasoning which followed. His observations were based on the experience of working in an office in which he had never wanted to work. He was making a good living at being unfulfilled. In weak moments he even found himself thinking that maybe it was not such a bad place. He would save for a mortgage and get his own place to live, buy a decent car, maybe develop a bit more ambition and responsibility. But was that his destiny?

While in this state-of-mind he found himself in the building's photocopying-cum-storage room later that morning. When he was feeling vexed, he would often take time to chill in the copier-storeroom situated off the open-plan office and away from his desk where he was surrounded by people, people, people. He would avoid the refreshment area – a corner of the floor with a kitchenette closed off by floor plants and chipboard partitions. He couldn't slip out onto the roof – the smokers' retreat; he could not even escape down the stairs and out into the car park because most of his break would be spent getting there and back. So, it was the copier-storeroom. He would make a coffee, grab a pile of carefully compiled copying jobs, roll his eyes at colleagues and mooch off to the small room. He would never turn down the opportunity to assist colleagues with their own photocopying. To some he had become a soft touch in this respect. Once ensconced in his refuge he would sit on a few boxes of copier paper, sip from his mug and photocopy as long as he dare.

Lost to his thoughts the minutes would just slide away as he stared at the patterns of wear in the carpet, the gentle whirr of the copier sweeping him away to a happier place. Once upon a time it was the sound of the Sirens' call that pulled men to their doom on the rocks, now it was the sound of the photocopier, the defining sound of life in the twenty-first century office.

Thus were his days stuffed into a blender; his existence turned into a tasteless mush...until that Tuesday morning when another sound was thrown into the mix. The sound of the copier was suddenly broken by the hard *rat-tat-tat* of something mechanical high above and behind him. Turning around, all he could see was a wall of shelving onto which was crammed stationery, boxes and antique office appliances.

It sounded like a woodpecker was breaking through from the other side of the wall. Maybe it was workmen drilling in short sharp bursts on the other side, he thought. What was on the other side of the wall? As far as he could recall it was a corridor.

The *rat-tat-tat* was immediately followed by the rustle of paper. Concerned, he quickly exited the storeroom and checked the corridor. Other than a few strange looks from colleagues, he saw nothing. He returned to the copier-storeroom to resume his coffee and study of the carpet. Knowing he had now been spotted, he cut short his break and finished up within a few minutes. Just as he was about to leave the room, it started again – some sort of *rat-tat-tatting* and paper rustling high up in the corner of the room.

What the hell? he thought. It's someone else's problem, if the building burnt down because of some severed electrical wire, so be it.

He returned to his desk to continue processing the company's business as his mind returned to his website project. He broke up the remainder of his work-day reviewing websites which tried to deliver the same functionality as his own had done, but none of them never really nailed it. Not in the way his website had done (or would have done if he had been able to follow it through to completion). It had been many months since the collapse of the project and the prospect of reviving it had fallen further and further away. Nevertheless, he was surprised that it did keep popping into his head. Surely that meant something? But he didn't have the time. He was a busy man. He would start the day with an early morning run, then work a full-day before leaving the building uninspired, even angry. He did not want to talk to anyone and so his evenings were spent exercising, watching movies, reading books on business start-ups and browsing the Internet all the while reliving the potential of the website project. Unfortunately, mobile applications or 'Apps' seemed to be all the rage now. Maybe websites had had their day.

– II –

There was no improvement the following week. The weekend had been lost to attempts to translate the website into an 'app' for mobile devices. Office work was the last thing on his mind, so whenever an opportunity came along to head to the copier-storeroom and photocopy, he took it. He laid the groundwork early in the morning by dropping references to a headache so that by mid-morning his offers to do his colleagues' photocopying did not arouse suspicion. Coffee made, he headed into the storeroom and took his seat on the boxes and set the copier running. Within moments he had adopted the carpet-staring pose he knew so well.

Then *rat-tat-tat* above and behind him.

He jumped up and spun round. Again, what the hell?

Silence. Nothing. What was up there? He couldn't see any dust that might have suggested there was some twit drilling in from the other side of the wall. Maybe there was a smoke alarm malfunctioning high up in the corner of the room behind those boxes. Whatever it was, it was annoying. What was the point of escaping to the storeroom if he was only to be disturbed by a *rat-tat-tat* hammering away? He sighed. Enough already, I'm having another ten minutes in here before I return to that damn desk, he thought, and sat back down.

No sooner had his breathing slowed when: *rat, rat, tat, buzz, tat, tat*.

He jumped up, stacked a handful of copier paper boxes on top of one another and, using the shelves as hand supports, climbed up towards the source of the rattle and buzz. Pushing aside boxes of stationery and trays of power cords and adaptors, he came across the cream-coloured side panel of a dirty, old electrical appliance tucked under other electrical accessories. Pulling gently, he dislodged the appliance from its lodgings. Its lead was still trapped down the far side of the shelf, but as he pulled the machine further towards him he recognised it as an old computer printer. One he had never seen in use. They were before his time, but he had seen them in films. *Rat-a-tat-tat* they went. The printer in his hands even had attached some of the old-style computer paper – green-lined with perforated sides. It was a dot matrix printer.

On such printers the print head ran back and forth across the paper rapidly hammering out dots that together became letters and eventually words. An office full of these old printers could not have been a pleasant place in which to work, he thought to himself as he tried to manoeuvre the machine from its resting place.

Was this the source of the noise? Still precariously balanced on the boxes, he gently pulled the antique towards himself only for the electrical power plug to snag between the shelf and the wall preventing further removal. With his thighs tiring under the strain he gave up and shoved the appliance back onto the shelf jumping down to safety but not before tearing off the printed pages.

Breathless by the only bit of exertion so far that day he read the handful of sentences.

Maybe what you seek is over the horizon.
So, raise your gaze and look.

And more sentences that must have been printed out the previous week:

What do you see?
What do you seek?
What do you see?

Bizarre. The printer wasn't connected to any network as far as he could tell. Perhaps a power surge had tripped the power unit in the printer kicking out a handful of messages held deep in its memory. He eyed the printer amidst the debris on the shelf above; it looked as if it had been buried up there for an age. The printer would have been sitting on the shelf undisturbed for at least six years and looked as if it had been retired many years before that. Laser printers had been standard in offices for nearly two decades.

The sentences looked less like a document and more like messages between colleagues. A pre-cursor to email perhaps – one colleague messaging another trying to cheer him or her up. Sweet. I wonder what happened to them, he thought. Did they marry and move away and are now blissfully unaware that their courtship by electronic mail was not lost in the ether and their messages were being printed out twenty, thirty years later on a malfunctioning printer? Ah, the wonders and romance of modern technology. Cheered by the thought that people had been connecting with each other even in an office environment, he left the room and returned to his desk.

'Headache better?' asked Sarah with an inquisitive smile snapping him back to his reality; thoughts of love in the ether banished.

– III –

His Fridays were not as cheerful as those in years past. The end of the working week had once induced cheer for it heralded a time for pubs, computer games, and, more importantly, the beginning of a forty-eight hour period in which he could work on his pet projects. Nowadays his Fridays were the precursors to forty-eight hours of 'opportunity-bleed'. So, his last visit of the week to the copier-storeroom was not made in the best of spirits.

He was watching the cloud formations and the battling of mythical beasts in the threadbare carpet when the *rat-tat-tatting* started above and behind him. He didn't move; his curiosity had been satisfied earlier in the week. So what if messages between long-dead lovers were being kicked out by a malfunctioning printer? What could he do with it? Nothing. Why take an interest in someone else's history of disappointments? It served no purpose. Besides the clouds and monsters were far more interesting. He'd let the power surge do its thing and let someone else discover the printouts and marvel at the quaintness of it all.

The racket stopped.

Lost deep in his thoughts it seemed as if the clouds were now moving. That was until a *rat-tat-tat* shattered the peace that had been settling upon him. Springing up, annoyed, he stepped up onto the boxes and, using the shelves once again to hold himself steady, reached up towards the printer and pulled. It seemed trapped fast. Perhaps one of its edges had slipped over the other side of the shelf when he replaced the printer a few days before. Giving up, he stepped back down on to the floor ripping a length of paper off the printer once again all the while refusing to admit to himself that he was curious. Any nonchalance was punctured by a dagger of disconcertedness when he read the printed text.

```
If what you seek is over a horizon,
why do you let your eyes fall?
A carpet may have clouds,
but no carpet has a horizon.
Lift your head. Raise your gaze.

A destination is not reached without motion.
Destinies do not move.
People do.
```

This didn't look like a conversation between lovers. This was personal. To him. Holy cow, he thought. I'm being played. Perhaps his colleagues had noticed that he had been spending perhaps too much time in the copier-storeroom and it was someone's bright idea to play a joke. There were contenders, including Gordon who might want him to look a bit of a fool. It might provide Gordon with a chance to be conspiratorial with Sarah thus getting a little closer to her. In fact, why had Sarah asked him about his headache the other day? A bit of misdirection? But, he then thought, am I coming across as someone who is pondering his destiny? They are playing me. How do they know I was looking at the carpet, he pondered? I wasn't aware I was doing it myself.

But, he reasoned, my copier-moments are interrupted and people do probably see me staring at the carpet. He calmed down. I mustn't succumb to their plan, he thought. I'll play it cool. They don't know the printer is working or that I am reading the printouts. I need to think about this.

He glanced up at the printer on the shelf above.

Perhaps I'll disconnect it then perhaps they might conclude their plan never worked and I never saw the printouts.

Just as he was about to step up on the pile of copier boxes to reach up for the printer and foil their plans, Jemima opened the door.

'Oh, have you finished?'

'Yes,' he said, stuffing the green printouts out of sight in his pile of 'photocopying' before exiting the room. He headed straight to his desk without looking in anybody's direction. He tried to recall how he might look when he usually exited the copier-storeroom and adopted as blank an expression as possible. He stuffed the green printouts in the lowest drawer of his desk and covered them with his waterproof jacket and worked harder in the remaining two-and-a-half hours that he had done for months.

At home that evening he could tell that the events of the day had unsettled him, because he couldn't shake them from his thoughts. He was irritated that he had somehow become the butt of an office joke, yet he was consumed by the printed words themselves. Sitting at his kitchen table, cooling coffee in hand, he stared at the words on the crumpled piece of paper.

```
If what you seek is over a horizon,
why do you let your eyes fall?
A carpet may have clouds,
but no carpet has a horizon.
Lift your head. Raise your gaze.

A destination is not reached without motion.
Destinies do not move.
People do.
```

How had they known he was seeing clouds in the carpet? Was it a lucky guess? The words had touched a nerve. Although he would never vocalize it, his 'destiny' was something that did preoccupy him. He knew the office was not, could not be, his destiny, but no sooner had he reached this conclusion, he doubted himself. For could a so-called 'destiny-not-realised' be described as a 'destiny'? In fact, was there a point at which one's daily existence became one's destiny? Surely all destinies were, by their very nature, realised?

```
Destinies do not move.
People do.
```

He studied the words. Destiny must be pursued?

Reflections aside, he had to think about more pressing matters – how was he going to manage this office-joke on Monday? He quickly dismissed the idea of not making visits to the copier-storeroom as that would confirm to the conspirators that they had been successful. Their devious prank had worked. He had 'been had'. No, he must continue as normal.

The weekend at home was, as expected, not much to write home about. He browsed the contents of biographies of entrepreneurs who had made their way in the world of the web. It was all a bit depressing.

He didn't make a visit to the storeroom early on Monday, but slipped into the room mid-morning hoping that he might be spared the gag. His colleagues were in a meeting, so he might be in the clear. Having sat there for ten minutes he thought he had got away with it, but just as he was about to take his last swig of coffee ….

Rattat-tat. Buzz buzz, rat-tat-tat.

He swore at his absent colleagues.

For all he knew they had installed a camera and were watching his reaction. The options were: finish his coffee and exit the room no doubt to howls of laughter in the office, or climb up, remove the offending printer and carry it out with him to howls of laughter. He concluded that walking out with the printer would be taking more control, besides it would be the end of the matter. If he didn't remove the printer from its place high up on the shelf, the next time he entered the room, even for a legitimate piece of copying, it would *rat-tat* away and the joke would continue. No, humiliating though it may be, he needed to remove the printer as well and endure the humiliation all at once.

Swigging the last of his coffee, he placed the mug on the copier and climbed up onto the copier boxes one final time. As he neared the dot matrix itself, it stopped. He imagined he could almost hear the laughter on the other side of the wall. The green printout spewed out by the printer hung down the side. He tore it away to make the removal of the printer easier. With a sigh, he gave into the temptation to read the printed words.

Apply yourself.

The words dug deep, their effect efficiently masked by his robust demeanor. Nobody in the office knew he had been as productive as a gnat. Nobody in the office knew about his website ambitions. It was sacred. His colleagues had just got lucky. Angry, he threw the paper down and grabbed the antique printer. He was expecting the first tug to free the appliance from its moorings. It didn't. His irritation merely energised subsequent tugs which resulted in the dislodging of other items from the shelf. Stationery and electrical accessories crashed down to the floor below, but it worked. He held the printer in his hands for the first time. One more yank would pull the power cord from behind the now semi-precarious shelf. What was unnerving was that the printer's power cord had not led to a plug secured in a wall socket. The door opened and Sarah entered.

'What the hell was that?' she asked her puzzled and distracted colleague.

'Oh nothing.'

'I heard a crash. What's going on?' she said as Gordon appeared behind her.

He looked at Sarah and Gordon searching hard for a suppressed smile, a hidden twinkle or a wobble in their serious faces. But nothing. Their bewilderment, concern was pure. Nevertheless, he offered up a wince, smile, frown, squint of 'I know what you're doing', but there was nothing in return. The fact that he held the unconnected power cord in his hand did not help matters.

His colleagues left, Gordon pulling a 'you're-an-office-weirdo' face, Sarah with a female equivalent and the words 'be careful'. And with that, he was left alone. He stepped down from the boxes and stood confused looking at the printer in his hands. He turned it over looking for accessories that might allow for network connectivity. Wi-fi. Bluetooth. Anything. But nothing. The printer itself pre-dated all such technology, that he knew. Unless his colleagues had gone to the considerable trouble of reconfiguring such an antique, there was no way the printer could connect to a network or 'operator'. He puffed and sighed. It must be some kind of spooky coincidence. He was reading too much into the printer's words. Dots of wisdom. Just a fluke.

He was snapped out of his contemplation by a colleague, Jane, entering and pointing at the photocopier. He waved her onwards and, tucking the printer away on a lower shelf out of sight, he slipped out of the room taking the green printer paper with him. He returned to his desk. It wasn't over. The matter required further investigation.

Save for a slight detour, he went straight home turning the events of the day over in his mind. Almost rebuking himself for doing so, he sat at the kitchen table staring at the 'how-to build a mobile app' book he had picked up from a bookseller on the little detour home. He pulled a small, blank, fresh notebook from his pocket and placed it open beside the book.

– IV –

The following day he was back in the office. This time he had no fear of going to the storeroom for a break. It had to be done. There was contemplation and photocopying to be done. The calmness that had descended upon him as a result of a productive evening had been immediately challenged by the news that a senior colleague was leaving the company to strike out on his own. The excitement that another person had seen a world beyond the plasterboard walls was swept away by the realisation that he could not afford to drop everything himself. If he did indeed hand in his resignation it would have to be for another job and that meant another office. Anything different would mean a significant drop in pay.

However, another thought, like a careful rat, was peeking out of the gloom and could not be ignored. With his colleague gone, there was the possibility that he might be promoted within months. The company was expanding and it was possible that he might be involved in managing part of the expansion of the office. A bit more money would mean funds for a mortgage and…. *rat-tat-tat, tat-tat, buzz, rat tat tat.*

He jumped out of his skin. Spinning around and looking up at the corner shelf, he instantaneously remembered than he had moved the printer to a lower shelf. Just as his eyes fell upon the profile of the printer under a few large sheets of paper, it fell silent. Now angry he pulled the dot matrix away from the shelf and dumped it hard on the work surface beside the photocopier. Its cord was not attached to a power supply, nevertheless he yanked the cord from the printer. It had no discernible means of power and he had no clue as to how it was receiving data. He read the two lines of text printed on the green-lined paper.

```
Why?
Why do that?
```

He didn't know what to think of it. He was annoyed that this little game was continuing. Jesus, why the hell couldn't .....
rat-tat-buzz-tat, tat-tat, buzz, rat tat tat.

The dot matrix starting printing right in front of him. He stared in total disbelief as the print head of this standalone, unconnected, antique printer whizzed back and forth rattling out more dots, more letters. The swirl of confusion, the hurt at the duping, the mocking of colleagues and anger at their persistence all dissipated when the printer came to a stop and the mechanism pushed up the paper into view.

```
If a destiny requires boldness, be bold;
If it requires action, act;
If it requires application, app
```

And then the words stopped. He was empty but for a quietness and a shallowness of breath. 'App'? Had it run out of ink? Had the Wif-fi connection been interrupted? Was 'apply' the word it had intended to print? 'Apply yourself.' It would make grammatical sense and the phrase had been used before. It must surely be the case because, as he kept reminding himself, no-one knew he was working on developing his website idea into an application or 'app' for a mobile device. No-one at all. His work environment was not that kind of place. He never shared such information or thoughts with colleagues, for that was what they were. Colleagues. Not friends. Sure, he might have an occasional drink with some of them, but he never shared his plans. When one is warmed by the flame of ambition, one should not share the heat.

How long he stood there looking at the damn machine he did not know. Like a gunfight in some dusty forgotten corner of the Wild West, someone had to blink first. The printer did.

Rat-tat- tat-buzz, tat-tat, buzz, rat-rat-tat.

```
Regret fills the vacuum of inaction.
Apply yourself.
Build it.
Things fail; Life succeeds.
Live not to fail but to prevail.
```

He looked at the lines over and over. He studied them in the hope that they were a fluke and could apply to any young man who might be unhappy at work and was looking for a way out. Maybe the words were just hitting home because the hoaxer(s) just got lucky. A part of him was almost pleading for him to see a phrase or a word that could not apply to him and his situation and so undermine this whole horrible situation. But it was not to be.

Rat-tat- tat-buzz, tat-tat, buzz, rat-rat-tat.

```
Fear has no future.
A cave has no light unless
a torch is carried deep therein.
```

He reached into his pocket and removed the small notebook in which he had written notes on the features for the app the previous night. It included a list of possible names for the app. The only one he had underlined was 'torchem'. It was an app designed for searching for obscure information on people and organisations. The sketched app button icon was a torch illuminating the darkness of a cave.

All he could hear was his heart beating, as if the organ itself was in suspense, waiting for his next move. He slowly lifted the printer, examined it once more for connectors, aerials and leads before gently replacing it on the work surface. With one sigh he ripped off the paper printout and, putting the printer under his arm, exited the room.

– V –

He timed his arrival close to the end of the day, that way he thought it might come across as more casual. He didn't know the IT officer well, but his role in the workplace required the IT man to take the request seriously. For nearly six hours he had sat at his workstation with the printer tucked under his desk doing little to no work. Every twenty minutes or so he opened his drawer to look at the latest printout. Although stunned by the events that morning, he was determined to be cool and calm just in case it was one hell of a hoax.

He almost felt sick when reflecting on the only two explanations. It was a joke which was working terribly and horribly well, or a genuine communication from 'what?', he did not know. His subconscious? A divine 'thing'? He couldn't use the word 'god'. Holy cow, maybe it was his destiny using some worm-hole to message him from the future? Or maybe it was just Gordon. Or Brian.

During the afternoon he had thought of all the possible ways a colleague or friend might have known about his interest and the app. He hadn't mentioned it, that he knew. In fact he hadn't mentioned it to anyone in that town. He had not browsed any website at work that in any way suggested an interest in the 'app' business. He was not an avid user of social media and wouldn't comment on such things even if he were. He hadn't made phone calls on the premises about such matters. He had bought a few items from on online reseller but that was all done from home. The embarrassed manner in which he had bought the book (in cash) about app-building would have prevented anyone reading its title. Not to mention the references to 'torch' and light and caves. So by the time he was standing in front of the T-shirt wearing IT officer at the IT reception desk he was pretty desperate to be told how it could be done.

'It's an old one. Where did you get this?' asked the bored technician.

'Oh, it was in a copier-storeroom place.'

'It's an antique.'

'It's printing out junk,' the visitor said, trying to move the conversation along. 'I thought maybe something was stored in its memory which is just being kicked out now.'

'These old printers don't have memory. Data was pushed straight from the network. It can't hold anything.'

'Maybe it's a Bluetooth thing,' the visitor replied determined to cover all options.

'Bluetooth?' the IT officer repeated with a look of total disgust. 'Bluetooth was developed in the mid-nineties. This piece of junk dates to the late-seventies, early eighties.'

'So, it wont be Wi-fi either....?' he murmured undeterred.

The IT technician started glancing around himself seemingly fearful that this was a set-up orchestrated by his own work colleagues. Recognising the man's behaviour as no different to his own in recent times, the visitor changed tack. He stopped himself from saying, 'It's just that it has been printing out messages and I think I might be the butt of some joke and I'd like to turn the tables,' because he suspected the IT officer might have sympathy for the colleagues and the gag.

'I'm part of a drama group that is putting on a play and we were hoping to use it as a prop.'

'What play?' asked the IT man.

Jesus, What? He's an 'effing IT officer, the visitor thought. Why would a computer nerd have any interest in play set in a 1980s office?

'The Hills Have Distant Memories, by Marjorie Wallace.'

It worked. The IT officer looked blank and the conversation moved on.

'But if it keeps kicking stuff out, it'll break the suspense,' the visitor continued.

'Of "The Hills Have Distant Memories"?' the officer said.

The visitor channelled all his conviction into the weakest of nods. 'I want to make sure it doesn't start printing during the play.'

'Well, just disconnect it from the mains.'

He didn't have the heart to tell the man that it was printing without power. 'Maybe there's still juice in its batteries?'

Nothing. Just a blank stare.

'Anyway, if you could check it over to see if there is any Wi-fi, Bluetooth, memory card malfunction, battery power unit thing.'

Still nothing. The visitor was now thinking of the pure and stress-less world beyond the door behind him.

'I'll owe you,' he said in a slightly deeper, cool voice attempting to make it an appealing offer, 'buy you a pint sometime.'

Nothing, which he took as a cue to leave.

The evening and the following day was spent in a degree of suspense. A visit to the copier-storeroom ended abruptly when he suddenly panicked and exited lest some other disconnected electrical appliance started jabbering away, but, no, all was quiet.

– VI –

At the close of the day, and with a degree of trepidation, he dropped by the IT department. On meeting the same IT officer he adopted a manner of world weariness as he casually enquired after the dot matrix. The stony-faced officer pulled the appliance from a shelf and lifted off the cover revealing the printer's insides. The visitor momentarily felt a pang of shock – surely the nerd hadn't broken it? Which made him think – was there a part of him that wanted it all to be true?

'Look, nothing. All antique. Certainly no memory. No battery,' the IT officer said waving at the appliance.

Scouring the insides of the printer, he could not see any piece of modern gadgetry, nothing that suggested a Bluetooth or Wi-fi capability. It all looked thirty years old.

'And it won't start printing in your play,' said the officer with a smug smile.

The visitor nodded. He had almost forgotten.

'Although technically no company property should leave the premises.'

'Right, I would return it straight away. Just a couple of weeks,' he said, trying to show deference to the expert – a deference the IT man desperately craved, he suspected.

Both elated and despondent, he collected the dot matrix in his arms and returned to his office. Thoughts of taking the printer home with him had crossed his mind, but he concluded it would be letting an unknown agent into his house. Besides, it would be far too unnerving if it started *rat-ta-ta-tatting* in his own home. So, he placed the machine in his desk cupboard and there it stayed for a few days. If it started printing again others would notice and it would become their problem too. As the days drifted by the printer preyed less on his mind. However, it was on the Friday evening that matters resurfaced.

He had planned to leave the office on time, but feedback on a report that had to be emailed overseas before the weekend landed on his desk with too many changes required to be done in a short space of time. He would be working until nine that evening.

When one is obliged to work late on a Friday, first there is anger then resentment and finally resignation. He knew he would lose the weekend just at a time when he was trying to bring about a new phase in his life. At 8.45 p.m. and with the document safely dispatched, he began to ruminate on his options. He had been making the final touches to a number of business plans for his project. He was also trying to complete an application for a ten-day business course in Internet startups. So the question hanging over him was: Should he hang back at the office and do the work staying to two or three o'clock in the morning? Or should he just go home and relax and hope he would summon the strength to do it over the weekend (in the full knowledge that he would not start anything until Sunday evening by which time he would feel rubbish and give up altogether)? The making of a quick coffee in the kitchenette would delay the decision-making for a few minutes at least, he concluded.

As he despondently stirred his drink the urge to head home crept closer. The office was empty and a certain peace had descended. The cleaners had been and gone. The lighting had been switched off and the open-plan office was now illuminated only by his desk lamp, a few weak ceiling spotlights and the light from nearby corridors spilling into the office. All was quiet. The only movement for two hundred yards in all directions was his swirling coffee. Another stir-and-a-half and his indecision morphed into a single word, 'whatever'. Who cares.

Rat-tat-tat.

The distant muffled sound snapped him out of his stupor. What the hell was that? he thought, knowing full well what it was. Surely not?

His pride fought with his curiosity. There was only ever going to be one winner. Leaving his coffee cooling, he weaved his way through the darkness towards his desk. Standing looking at the cupboard under his desk, he knew what lay within. With a flash of resolve he opened the cupboard, removed the dot matrix printer and placed it on his chair with a clear view of its 'disconnectedness'. One line.

You care.

Moving the chair and its precious cargo to the middle of the office and away from interference, he returned to the kitchenette and continued to slowly stir his coffee, his ear fully alert to any sound. Stay or go, stay or go. Stay or go? He repeatedly pushed the question through his mind. Stay or go, stay or go.

Rat-tat-tat.

He looked over at the chair and printer thirty feet away illuminated by a spotlight embedded in the ceiling. Cucumber cool, he strolled over to the chair, coffee in hand. Coming to a stop in front of the printer he looked at the appliance like a parent to an errant child and read the one word printed on the antique green-lined computer paper.

Stay.

His heart didn't skip a beat, it seemed to cease beating altogether. His brain didn't explode in fireworks nor cloud over with confusion, his mind was sky-blue clear. Placing the dot matrix back in the cupboard, he sat down at the computer and worked through to nearly 4.00 a.m. the following Saturday morning. He submitted the application for the ten-day course along with the bursary application for the course fee, finalised different versions of the business plan for different audiences, placed submissions and enquiries on community noticeboards for guidance and appeals for possible collaboration. He wasn't excited, he wasn't inspired, he wasn't emotional. He was just methodical. If he noted anything as he worked, it was the absence of doubt. At 3.53 a.m. he sent an email to an old friend who worked in a local hospital proposing a meeting fifteen hours later at 7.00 p.m. on Saturday evening and calling in a favour. With that he logged out, closed down, packed the dot matrix into his bag and left the office. He was home by 5.00 a.m. and went straight to bed in the full knowledge that there would be no panic on Sunday evening. Everything he could do, had already been done.

– VII –

On Saturday evening he walked into the local hospital and met his old friend, a doctor. They slipped downstairs to X-ray department and placed the dot matrix in the machine. Images from different angles were taken, viewed and a diagnosis was offered. The images were converted into electronic files that he took away with him.

Freed from project work over the weekend, he spent the Saturday evening sitting in front of his computer studying the X-ray image files of the dot matrix printer and compared it to any picture and printer manual he could find on the Internet. His eager eye examined every pixel of the image. Nothing seemed untoward. Every wire and component was accounted for. The IT officer had verified the printer from an IT point of view. The X-rays had shown that there were no hidden compartments, wires or aerials. The dot matrix was in the clear, as he had suspected. Tired, he made a sandwich, drank some juice and fell asleep watching one of the 1980s mullet-headed action movies that had now become a classic.

He rose from the sofa in the dark hours of Sunday morning and returned to his room to sleep a few more hours before the day began. Looking at the antique dot matrix sitting next to its pristine laser descendant on his desk, he appreciated the wisdom hidden deep in its heavy plastic frame and clumsy functional design.

I'll return the printer to the copier-storeroom later that day, Sunday, he thought. He wanted a break from the company of the dot matrix. It wasn't that he wasn't grateful, he most certainly was. He just didn't want reminders of his working week to be visited upon him on that particular Sunday. In fact, while he was in the office, he could fire off a few more emails and business plans. His Sunday evening might be the first in many, many months when he wouldn't feel that he had wasted the previous forty-eight hours. So, as he turned off the light and rested his head on the pillow, he quietly thanked the dot matrix for its insight and words of support.

His eyes were closed for no more than thirty seconds before the familiar whirr and buzz of the unconnected printer started and *rat, tat-tat-tatted* for ten seconds. There was no panic. He almost greeted the disturbance like an old friend. Tired and comfortable, he didn't want to move, but he knew he wouldn't sleep until he had answered the printer's call. What it had to say, he didn't know. Everything had been said. So with a sigh and heave, he crawled out of bed and turned on the desk lamp. One line.

After the darkness, comes the light.

Nice. A joke? A tease? Or more solemn philosophising? With the faintest of smiles and the lightest of nods, he turned off the light and returned to bed. Like a kiss goodnight he thought to himself.

He rose the next morning, Sunday, placed the printer in the bag and headed off to his workplace stopping for a cooked breakfast on the way. The office was quiet, empty. With a quiet reverence, he returned the dot matrix to the exact same place on the shelf in the copier-storeroom. Who knows maybe it would continue to print messages of support during his upcoming visits, but, perhaps more importantly, it should be given the chance to print messages for other visitors. He carefully laid a spare piece of printer paper over it to shield it from view and left to work for a few hours at his desk. He dispatched more emails, read blogs, and registered his own blog. He joined a crowd-sourcing website designed to raise small amounts of capital for small-time entrepreneurs. With that done, he left and headed home. Everything he could have done that weekend, he had done indeed, and then some.

– VIII –

On Monday he sailed back into the office a tired but rejuvenated man. It was mid-morning when the email arrived. It was from the course organisers he had emailed late on Friday. They regretted that he had not been successful in being allocated a place on the course running the following month, it was full. Furthermore, the bursaries had been allocated for the two subsequent courses. So far, so disappointing. But the email continued. It just so happened that there was a place on a course that started mid-morning on that day (Monday) as one of the (bursary-supported) participants had dropped out. So, the email read, if he could get himself to central London, the course providers would be happy for him to complete the ten day course using the now-available bursary funds. The half-day that he would miss would be covered by the course provider during the course or even at the end of the course.

It was a no-brainer. He was stunned, then jolted. A colleague had tapped him on the shoulder.

'Richard wants to see you.'

Richard was hardcore administration. Nice timing, he thought as he headed to Richard's office, I can let him know I am taking the next ten days off. No buts, or ifs. He wasn't stupid, he wasn't going to wave this opportunity away.

The purpose of the meeting soon became clear.

'We're expanding and a couple of jobs that have been pending are being confirmed this morning. I think it is time for you to move to the next stage and we'd like to offer you a role in managing one of the projects. It's more money, career progression.'

With his head consumed by the growing excitement of the course, he said nothing. Richard assumed the reaction was owing to the growing excitement of promotion.

'Richard, thanks, but something's come up, I have an opportunity to go on a course for ten days, from today.'

'That was quick,' Richard replied, confused.

'Just come through, someone dropped out of a course. I won't be here tomorrow and will be back Thursday next week.'

'What is it?' asked Richard.

He did a quick calculation. The approval of holiday leave was not in the bag. He had to be compliant in some way.

'It is career progression. IT skills and commerce.'

'Who's paying for it?' asked Richard suddenly concerned that he had not approved any course. Richard had never considered his colleague to be the type of person who would fund his own career development.

'The Government. I applied for a course a couple of months hence. Didn't get it, but they've just emailed and said if I come today, I can get a bursary-funded place. I'll forward you the email.'

'OK,' mumbled Richard, suddenly cornered. He didn't want to lose his first choice of manager. It wouldn't look good to the boys upstairs. 'We can talk when you're back. In the meantime, we will have some reorganisation out there,' Richard said nodding towards the open-plan office.

'Fine. Feel free to move me anywhere.'

'We may have you sharing an office with Derek.'

'OK,' he said, almost beginning to think there might never be a time when he would share an office with Derek.

With that he rose and exited with an energy and enthusiasm that Richard also misread. Back at his desk he sent an email accepting the course place saying he hoped to get there by mid-afternoon, phoned the course organisers confirming the same and lastly forwarded the email to Richard editing out the words that might suggest the course wasn't entirely dovetailed to the day job. Grabbing his coat and bag, he headed out the door without stopping. I say 'without stopping', he did slow down as he passed the copier-storeroom door and tipped his hat to the ally within. Proper thanks would come later.

–IX–

He returned to the office on Thursday of the following week. For years he had approached his workplace as if the building itself was an obstacle that blocked his path, obscured his horizon. On this particular day, one of his last, it was almost translucent.

The course had finished the previous day and, after a night out with the other course attendees, he had arrived home late only to spend a few hours updating documents and forwarding them to new contacts. He had allowed himself a little lie-in and was therefore reaching the building shortly after 10.00 a.m.. Spotting the fire-exit doors open at the rear of the building he thought he would slip up the back stairs to his desk rather than endure the looks of disapproval from the reception and office staff. He marvelled at a skip full of office equipment and furniture at the fire-exit and was reminded of Richard's plans to push through office rearrangements in his absence. Ten days ago was a lifetime.

It's all change, he thought.

He raced upstairs and slipped into the office to find that there had indeed been a substantial rearrangement of furniture and personnel. At least a dozen additional desks had been squeezed onto the floor. Desk partitions and disconnected computers littered the office. New faces hung around chatting, looking like lambs to the slaughter. Just when he thought he had found his desk, he was stopped by one of his junior colleagues, Ele.

'I think they've moved you in with Russell,' she said nodding towards the other end of the office.

There was one particular task he wanted to complete before spending time with Russell, but he was unable to find a working computer. He weaved his way through the desks and found his new office. Thankfully Russell was absent, but his new office was in a similar state of disarray. He sat at his desk attached to which a few of his yellow post-it notes remained, reminding him of a past life. A formal email of resignation to Richard was not possible. Even the old-school method of a letter was not possible because there was no printer attached to the end of any cable. He had relished the thought of his first task of the day being the dispatch of a date-stamped resignation letter from his office email account. Disappointment at a possible delay soon turned into a warm realisation that there was possibly a poignant resolution to his difficulties. What could be more appropriate than printing a resignation letter on his old friend, the dot matrix? Assuming, he thought to himself with a chuckle, the dot matrix hadn't already printed out the letter for him.

With the first genuine smile he had broken in that office for years he jumped up and bounced back through the maze of furniture to his old favourite haunt, the copier-storeroom noting that if he did stay in the job he would not be able to escape to the storeroom quite so often. Flinging open the door in readiness to greet an old friend his eyes were met with an empty room. He blinked in disbelief in the vain hope it would make a difference. He looked up towards the corner of the room where the dot matrix printer had waited for him in quiet wisdom for all those years only to see an expanse of dirty white walls. Not only was the dot matrix not to be seen, but the shelves themselves had been dismantled. The boxes of copier paper were nowhere to be seen. There was no suggestion that stationery had ever resided in that room. Even the bulky photocopier had been removed.

He stepped backwards out of the room in shock before stopping a colleague, who he thought was called Mary, in the corridor. Struggling to gather his senses he asked what was going on?

'They're turning it into an office,' Mary or Maria replied, wholly unaware of the gravity of the situation.

'Where's the printer?' he gasped, before adding as an afterthought, 'and the copier. And other stuff.'

Miriam (was that her name?) nodded down the corridor. He turned to see the copier plugged into the wall in the corridor. Stationery and copier boxes were stacked up beside it.

'But where's the dot matrix?' he asked desperately, figuratively grabbing his colleague by the lapels and shaking her.

'What?' she replied, figuratively slapping him across the face in disgust. 'I don't know, ask IT. They were clearing the room out.'

He spun round with the wild, desperate expression all too often seen when IT support was required. In his mind's eye he raced back through time and his arrival at the building. He had seen IT officer. But where? On the stairs talking to another IT man? He ran back to the stairwell and down to the ground floor passing various builders and fitters ferrying office furnishings back and forth.

He burst out into the daylight.

'The printer. I need the printer,' he said racing up to IT officer standing at the open doors of a delivery van.

'We'll get you set up within a few hours.'

'The dot matrix.'

'No, you'll have a fancy new laser printer,' the IT man said nodding towards the van full of boxes.

'No, it's the dot matrix I want. For the play….,' he said trailing off.

'"Memories of Marjorie's mams"?'

'Yes,' he blurted out, knowing full well it wasn't but not having the slightest idea what he had said two weeks before.

'That was two weeks ago.'

'I know. Re-runs,' he said weakly.

The IT officer gave up and nodded towards something over the shoulder of the recently promoted office-drone whose body was beginning to shake.

The pale man turned and looked. All he could see was an empty car park bordered by a road full of traffic. He spun back trying to communicate anger in his carefully staged glare. It didn't move the IT officer who just nodded more specifically towards the road.

He spun round again, his eyes scouring the horizon. What was it? There was nothing but traffic backed up at a traffic light. What could possibly be…..

Then he saw it. The lorry. And on its back, a skip.

He spun back.

The IT officer nodded.

His stomach plummeted forty storeys to the reinforced concrete of a basement car park. He looked. The lorry must be four hundred yards away. He was young, but he wasn't fit. He raced off towards the lorry.

'Luvvies,' the IT officer muttered shaking his head before turning his attention to the van full of lifeless laser printers.

No sooner had he covered thirty yards when the traffic lights turned green and the skip lorry with its sacred mystery buried deep within started to move off. Thinking he had half-a-mile of sprint in his legs, he disappeared from view waving and shouting. It was a full fifteen minutes before his hunched, drooping figure reappeared in the car park.

The IT officer took pity on him. 'Can't interest you in a HP260?' he said pointing to a broken, old, inkjet printer at his feet.

Exhausted by the unexpected exertion, he ignored the jibe and slowly made his way back into the building and his new office. He sat in silence, lost in thought. After a while he stirred into action and picked up the phone. He tracked down the individual who had hired the company and then the company itself and then a phone number. He made a phone call and negotiated his way through the switchboard to someone who could make a decision at the other end. All the while he was becoming more despondent and incredulous at himself for going to such lengths to rescue an antique electrical appliance, but deep down he knew that the dot matrix's mission had been completed. It had fulfilled its own destiny. Perhaps it had sat patiently on the top shelf for thirty years waiting for its moment to come. It had. And now it had gone. The course he had attended had hit the mark in terms of his needs. He had made contacts and joined a collective of start-ups. A small amount of crowd-sourcing funds had come through and a local business angel was interested in developing the app. He had secured a small loan himself and calculated that he could survive for nine months. The app would be up and working within eight weeks. He had twelve days left to work in the office taking into account the holiday leave entitled to him. He was free. He was happy. He was home.

The person at the other end of the phone informed him that the skip would be going to a depot and its contents crushed. It could be delayed for twenty-four hours, at a cost of £850 plus VAT. The skip itself was required elsewhere.

It was the silent crash of stage curtains on his drama with a dusty printer. Ahh, the brutality of swishing velvet. The end.

Now that he was handing in his notice, he could not afford £1,000 from his precious cash reserves. He dragged his thoughts away from the printer and towards the resignation letter on the screen in front of him. He must move forward. Who knows, maybe the dot matrix, or whatever it was, would print its way out of its predicament. As he forced himself to tap away on a newly-acquired keyboard, he wondered if he was the only one. There must be others, surely? Perhaps in some corner not very far away, he mused, there was a flush-faced woman staring in disbelief at the message generated by her own disconnected, antique, office appliance....?

Scary Afternoon in the Garden

– I –

We had been told to stay indoors when this happened. It had never happened to us before, but I know my mum and dad had spoken to other families in the town who had been visited by the creatures. One boy about my age had been killed, though I think that that was his fault. It was still scary though. I did worry a little but I knew that I was more responsible. After all, I was a bit older. (I was technically eleven, but I felt twelve.) I know my mum and dad thought I was a responsible person. I was nearly a man and I didn't really answer back unless I knew they were wrong and I had proof. I wanted a responsible job when I grew up – something that involved danger. I knew I had to practice dealing with danger now and develop my responsible instincts. Besides, it was good to develop a responsible reputation so that when I applied for all the dangerous jobs I could point to my life as a boy and say, 'Look, I was responsible then when lots of boys are irresponsible, that proves I will be responsible now. As a grown-up.' I think it would make quite a convincing argument.

I had thought of being a soldier – I knew it was dangerous work firing guns and that you had to be responsible – but my mum always went silent whenever I mentioned it and I knew that silence meant she was worried. I didn't want her to worry. She was sometimes worried when stuff wasn't serious. I knew she wasn't seriously worried because she wouldn't go quiet, but whenever I mentioned growing up and being a soldier (sometimes I was asked by an aunt or a visiting family friend) my mum would always go quiet. Sometimes she would fidget. I never talked about it to make her worry on purpose or to shut her up. I was never that mean, besides, it would not have been responsible.

I suppose she wouldn't have worried if there wasn't a war going on. Then it would have been just a normal boy's normal dreams of having an exciting life as a grown-up. It wasn't a big war, but it was in a very far away place. In a country with some deserts and even some jungles. To tell you the truth if I were ever going to be a soldier I wouldn't want to fight in the deserts or the jungle. Too hot in the desert and too sticky in the jungle. I didn't tell my mum this though.

I used to see some of the soldiers around town, near the shops. They seemed nice. Their uniforms were very smart. Sometimes there were little parades as they marched off to war. Local people would turn out and wave flags and cheer. My mum and dad never went though. My dad always seemed embarrassed when he saw the soldiers. Maybe it was because he felt he should have been a soldier himself, but he was far too old. I think he was quite fit though and he certainly wasn't fat. In some ways it was good that he wasn't there that afternoon in the garden because he might have been killed. In fact, he definitely would have been killed! It was probably a good thing I was by myself, which was strange because it was only the second time I had been left in the house all alone. I didn't find it scary being left on my own. It felt responsible. And that was good.

– II –

I will try to explain the lay-out of the house and the garden because I think it is a very important part of this story. We lived in a suburb of Oxonville in a road called Eboracum Road. We lived at number twelve, nextdoor to number ten where our neighbours lived. They were semi-detached houses built just after the fourth big war. We didn't have any houses opposite us, there was just a patch of waste ground, called Rocky Edge. It would be a great place to play, but it was fenced off with the razor wire because the grown-ups thought it was dangerous. There were no creatures there so I don't know why they thought it was dangerous. I have played there secretly with my friends once before. It was exciting, but I felt guilty and worried that it was not responsible, so I haven't done it again. (Not yet, but I might, but not just yet.)

We live on the outskirts of Oxonville. The area is quite new. There isn't much beyond the end of our garden, just some old farm buildings, fields and then the Overshot Woods begin about half-a-mile away. They say that people are going to build streets behind us (between us and the woods) and make number ten Eboracum Road a corner. That new road will be called Eboracum Avenue. I don't want houses at the bottom of my garden, but nobody asks me. If there had been houses at the bottom of my garden then things might have been different that day.

Our house had one front room downstairs and a back room and kitchen at the back of the house. The back room was quite dark so the builders attached a glass conservatory on the back of the back room (if you know what I mean). The conservatory was full of light and made the garden look very near. When mum, dad and my little sister moved there (into the house), my mum and dad thought the glass walls and roof of the conservatory were not strong enough. So they got builders to add two extra thick layers of glass. This was because of the danger! I'm very glad now that they did add two layers of glass and not one layer.

Upstairs there were two normal-sized bedrooms, a smaller slim one (bedroom) and a bathroom, but they're not important to the story. Outside the conservatory there was a concrete area and a laundry wheel. (A laundry wheel is a wheel that spins on the top of the metal pole and you can hang wet clothes on the wires that hang between the spokes of the wheel).

Then there was a long brick garage (with a small window) on the left hand side of the garden as you looked down the garden (towards the woods) from the conservatory. Along the side of the garage was a flowerbed that ran all along the garage wall. Next to the flowerbed was a long concrete path that went all the way to the end of the garden. Beside the path was a long slim lawn about ten feet wide that also ran to the end of the garden. Next to that was a very slim flowerbed and wire fence (as tall as my dad) running all the way to the end of the garden. Mostly it was all grass. Here's a likeness:

I should have said it was a long slim lawn with a slim flowerbed and wire fence on the right side and a wider flowerbed and garage on the left side. That would have been clearer. The garage went half way down the garden. After that was another bit of grass. I say grass, it was grass underneath all the cuttings and garden waste piled up high (again as tall as my dad). A fallen tree at the end of the garden hid an old greenhouse that was falling to bits. Somebody might have used the greenhouse to grow vegetables, but stopped – probably when a creature visited.

What was good was that the garden waste, the fallen tree and the fence gave the garden some protection from intruders. That was the point. It was a plan. We couldn't afford electric fencing around the whole garden so my mum and dad thought natural overgrown gardening rubbish would do the job. Most of the people in the area didn't have modern electrical fencing. Some did. We didn't. We wouldn't need it, we thought. The creatures normally stayed in the woods.

– III –

It all started on a Tuesday. In the afternoon. It was half-term so I wasn't at school. My dad was in the office that day. He was planning to take Wednesday and Thursday and Friday off work to play with us. We were going to have a special meal that night to celebrate the half-term break (from school) as a family because dad would be there, but mum had forgotten some ingredients. We had just had a sandwich lunch when mum said we needed to go to the shops to get the missing ingredients. (I can't remember what they were.) Normally I would be grumpy but I would go just to keep her happy. My dad said I should always try to keep my mum happy. Once I was grumpy myself and said to him, 'isn't that your job? You married her.' Then he looked grumpy. I don't know if it was because I answered back, or because it was true.

'You will get married one day,' he replied. 'So it would be good to get some practice in.'

I understood what he meant, but I still think he was making excuses and trying to manipulate me, but I let it go.

Even though the shops were only five minutes away in the motorized vehicle we would never walk. We had been told not to walk for the last year. Our road was not protected yet. Maybe in a few years, they said. Apparently, because of the war there were not enough worker-men to do the work. Also, things like metal were needed for the war, so the fences could not be built and because Overshot Woods were so close to our garden, people thought we might not have time to react quickly if a creature emerged from the trees. I told my mum and dad that I was one of the fastest runners in my class and even if something came out of the woods and started to cross the field towards the end of our garden, I would still have time to run back into the house even if I were at the bottom of the garden. Both my mum and dad looked grumpy and then my dad said I would always have to be looking out towards the woods which wouldn't be much fun. Then my mum said if I was having fun in the garden I wouldn't be thinking about the woods. Then my dad pointed out that I was assuming there wouldn't be any fog or mist or rain or something. Or that the daylight would be good. I was going to ask them 'why would I be playing in the rain or at night?' because, as I said earlier, that wouldn't be responsible, but then my mum came out and nailed it.

'It wouldn't be responsible of us to let you play down at the end of the garden until we have proof that you can run faster than anything that came out of the woods,' she said.

I suppose this is why grown-ups run the world, because they can think of intelligent things to say to children. God, I can't wait until I grow up more! I couldn't say anything because I had lost to Gary Murphy in a race at break-time the week before. I always beat Gary so it was a shock when he beat me. I think it was because he was growing faster than I was and his legs were longer. When my next growing spurt comes along and my legs get longer I think I will beat him again. I certainly didn't think I was getting shorter or slower. It was because of this that I lost that argument with my mum. I was a little annoyed because she had pulled out the 'responsible' argument knowing it was something I usually did. It was clever and annoying. According to my friends mums can be like that.

Anyway, back to the story. Tuesday afternoon. My mum gave in to my pleas for me to stay at the house. I used the 'responsible' line and also a new tack – the word 'trust' that she had used in the past. She kissed me goodbye (why, I don't know, she was only going to be away for twenty minutes) and bundled my little sister into the automobile. I closed the front door and went straight back into the house and the back room. I pulled up a chair in front of the sliding Franks door and looked out through the double layers of reinforced glass in the conservatory. I opened the sliding Franks doors a little. They were heavy and I knew that the glass was strong. We didn't really need the conservatory. I returned and sat down on the stool and looked out down the garden and out towards the field over the wall and the woods beyond. I imagined sprinting down the garden touching the wall and running back. I guessed that it would take twelve seconds to run from the conservatory down to the wall. It would be good training. Maybe then I'd beat Gary Murphy. I thought if mum went to the shops every day, I could run up and down the garden six times every day, so that when I got back to school I would certainly be able to beat Gary Murphy even though my legs hadn't grown much during half-term.

As I was thinking about this and calculating the number of times I should practise running up and down the garden, something suddenly jumped up on the wall at the end of the garden. It was strange because everything else in my line of sight remained the same except suddenly there it was, standing on the wall. I hadn't even seen it cross the field. Maybe it had crossed the field out of view (towards a neighbour's house – number eight or number fourteen) and then walked along the edge of the field until it reached our wall. Then jumped on it.

I froze. My eyes remained locked on the creature in case it jumped back down again out of view and disappeared back across the field into the woods, but it stayed there for a few seconds just looking left and right. I moved my eye to the left towards the fallen tree and the greenhouse and back to the creature. I was trying to calculate how tall the creature was. It was over half as tall as the greenhouse, I estimated, and about as tall as the fallen tree-trunk's half-way point. (The tree-trunk wasn't flat on the ground as all its branches were lifting it diagonally off the ground.) According to my calculations that made it about the same size as my dad, maybe a little taller. (And my dad was of average height, although he didn't like it when my mum described him as average height or 'average' in anything. I thought 'average' was good, it means normal, not very weird, unremarkable.) Although I hadn't really seen a creature so close before with my own eyes, I could tell it was a dangerous one.

I didn't know it's name off by heart which annoyed me – I should have studied harder, but how was I supposed to know which creature would appear in our garden? I thought about the book sitting on the bookshelf in my room. The book had drawings and descriptions. One part of me wanted to run upstairs, grab the book and bring it downstairs, but I knew the creature would probably disappear while I was away. So, I thought what would a teacher, an explorer or even my dad do? I concluded that they would remember a description of the animal in their heads and write it down properly afterwards and then compare it with the books later. Although I did realise that teachers, explorers and maybe even my dad wouldn't do this because they would know what creature it was anyway. So this is my description of the animal that I wrote down in my head. I kept adding to it, but I shall start from its feet up, because I thought a person would normally look at the head and not the feet, so I thought I should force myself to look at the feet and legs otherwise I would forget.

It has two feet. The feet look a bit like a horse's hooves but with long curled nails, three perhaps, with the biggest in the middle. Maybe a bit like an eagle's talons. A hoof, but like a claw. Or a talon. The middle claw-talon could move all by itself. In the same way a person can move his fingers without moving them all together at once. It wasn't like my own toes. 'Independently' is the word I think I am looking for, I think. Apparently this middle toe-claw (which could move independently) was the most dangerous bit about the creature. I overheard an old man saying that it was the middle toe-claw that caused the main injuries on the boy who was killed the year before.

– IV –

I had heard grown-ups talking about the death of the boy. They always whisper as if children have super-special hearing. But if we have super-special hearing, why whisper? We'd hear them anyway. I think that is what they call 'logic'. They say that if logic is involved it means the argument is always right, but I am not sure, because my mum and dad say they use logic a lot. (They do with me, anyway.) But if logic is always right, then they would never be wrong, but they are, so many times. There was this time when my mum used to tell me to stop slamming doors around the house. I never did slam a door in the house. Ever.

'Oh, was it the ghost?' my mum would say. Then she would say the slamming doors had to be me because all the ghosts had left the house when we moved in. Everyone else (i.e. her, my dad and my little sister) was downstairs therefore it had to be me slamming the doors. It was logic, she said. I think she was also being sarcastic, but I couldn't be sure, because being sarcastic is the opposite to being logical. (I didn't know if you could use both together at the same time. Surely one would cancel out the other?)

I sort of knew ghosts didn't exist, but I couldn't prove it at the time, so I didn't want to use logic in case it wasn't a good thing to back up my argument and undermined my case. I needn't have worried though, because my time would come. And it did. I learned to be patient.

My time came when we were all sitting around the dining table downstairs having tea a month later. We were eating and chatting happily when suddenly there were two loud bangs – two doors had slammed upstairs. Playing safe I decided not to say I was using logic, because I wanted to be sarcastic. I cleverly said sarcastically, 'sorry for slamming the doors'.

My mum squinted at me. I knew she didn't know what to say. Whatever she said, she wouldn't be able to say she was using logic.

'Perhaps it was the wind,' said my dad with a little smile, 'this time'.

My mother turned to me. 'Perhaps you shouldn't leave the doors open.'

'Perhaps it was the ghosts coming back to the house,' I said.

'Um,' she said back, squinting her eyes.

It was a stale-mate. We both knew neither of us could use logic. She wanted to save it for a time when she was lacking all the facts again. Then it hit me – I realised that logic depended on facts, but if not all facts are known then logic cannot back up an argument, and, because we never know all the facts, we (or rather my mum) cannot use logic to win an argument. Ever.

Anyway, the boy lived down the street. He was younger than me and not as responsible. I wanted to speak to his friends about his gruesome death. I was always polite, but I thought as I was responsible I had to be careful when asking questions. I had watched grown-ups and how they tried to gather information in a roundabout way when someone had died. It must be frustrating asking questions when really you want to hear answers to different questions. Doesn't seem logical to me. But then, as I have explained, logic is for confused adults. Anyway I tried it (not asking the questions I wanted answered), so I never said, 'tell me, how did he die?' How did the creature kill him?' and, 'was there much blood? Did he scream a lot? How loud?'

I used phrases that I heard old people say: 'I feel for your loss,' and 'my thoughts are with you at this difficult time.' It didn't work though. I just got odd looks from his friends and they didn't tell me anything, so I gave up and asked the questions straight: how did he die? Did the creature eat him? What bits of him did the creature eat? Did the creature look as if it was enjoying its meal? Did it drink the boy's blood? How much blood was there? Did it spurt? How far? And many more.

I learned that you can waste a lot of time as an adult – asking questions. Maybe that is why grown-ups have so many years growing old and rubbish (when I say 'rubbish' I mean rubbish at walking, running, shouting, and sometimes even speaking properly). They need all that time to ask all those questions and utter phrases that are of no interest to anyone. That is not to mention the years they need answering questions from other people. Truth is, at times, I was not looking forward to growing up and wasting so much of my life. After all life can be short. Especially if a creature wants to eat you.

I got the answers I wanted. The boy had been kicking a ball against a garden wall that was supposed to be high enough to keep out the creatures. One time he kicked the ball that hit the edge of a protruding buttress which knocked it upwards. The ball got stuck between a tree branch and the wall. He tried to use a stick to dislodge the ball but he only managed to push it deeper into the tree's branches. So he climbed halfway up the tree and tried again with a short stick. (Because sometimes short sticks are better.) He climbed higher and tried harder. Then apparently (said a friend who had been watching from the next door garden and telling him to stop because it was dangerous) the boy dislodged the ball from the branches. It dropped, bounced on to the top of the wall and then bounced down into the field on the other side of the wall.

The boy climbed on to the top of the wall itself and looked over into the field for the ball. That was when the creature got him. It jumped up grabbed his head in its mouth and pulled him down into the field. There was a little bit of screaming, but not much. (I don't know why. Maybe he was scared or maybe it was because his head was in the creature's mouth and the screams were muffled.) Luckily it didn't bite the boy's head off. The boy's head was still attached to his body when they found him so his family could bury him in one piece, which was good news. However, there was a big gash in his body from his neck to his tummy.

They think the creature used one of its feet to hold the boy down by the neck and, like a can opener, used the middle talon of the other claw to cut him open in one big movement. There was lots of spurting blood because blood was found on the wall. Some his friends told me the blood is still there on the wall, although it is much darker now because it is not fresh. Nobody has cleaned it off the wall probably because nobody can see it (including his mother) because it is on the field-side of the wall. Grown-ups only get worked up about things they can see. 'It is behind closed doors.' In this case it's because it is on the field-side of the wall.

The boy was obviously very tasty because most of his insides were eaten. At least he didn't die for nothing. For a few weeks afterwards I worried that the creatures might develop a taste for boys and come back, but I soon forgot about it.

There was a lot of screaming much later, but that was the boy's mum when she was told what had happened. It doesn't really count because she was not the one who was killed and eaten. I think if a woman were attacked the screaming would be a lot better. After the attack the parents didn't let any of the children play in the garden and there was lots of pressure on the local authorities to build the fence and higher walls. There was talk of going into the woods to find the creature and any other creature. The mothers of young children were keen, but when they tried to find volunteers, people were busy. Other things changed too. Life got more exciting. Some of the bigger boys used to play dares near the end of their gardens and a siren was installed in every street. Anybody could run out into the street and pull the lever to start the siren if a creature was seen in the field or leaving the woods. This made some people angry because they said there should be a lever in everyone's house. Some people tried to form a watch-group with a timetable to watch the woods and field from their upstairs bedroom windows, but people got bored. The grown-ups kept reminding us of the lessons we should have learnt. They said when the ball got stuck, the boy shouldn't have climbed higher and tried harder. It is true what they say: If at first you don't succeed, it is probably best to stop. In case you get eaten. And: Perseverance can lead to a horrible death.

They think the ball hitting the wall caught the creature's attention and it made its way across the field from the trees.

That's why playing with balls in gardens was banned in case it attracted the attention of the creatures in the woods. So, I never played with a ball in my garden. That is why I could only run around. The boy had been killed the previous year so it was a long time ago. I heard that the mother missed her son every day, but although I thought about it every day for a while, in time it became a memory of an event which might one day find its way into a history book written by someone who was never there. Historians are clever – they can write about stuff they've never experienced themselves (and get lots of credit for it).

I didn't worry that it was going to happen to me because not one person referred to the boy being (or wanting to be) responsible. Perhaps it doesn't matter that he died because he was not going to be responsible when he grew up. (And that might have been even more dangerous for him and other people.)

– V –

Back to the description of the creature in my garden. Its calves were strong and muscly, so were its thighs – much more than a man's. And much, much more than my dad's. This was because the creature was probably always running around for food. Maybe in the past men's thighs were just as muscly, but when men started growing food on farms and then having food in shops, they did less running around. I'm not saying shopping isn't tiring. My mum always huffs and puffs when she comes home with lots of shopping and says she is tired, but I think that is a different kind of tiredness. I find shopping very tiring. No sooner have we started shopping I want to lie down and sleep, sometimes even die. My dad's thighs aren't muscly but he doesn't do much shopping so we'll never know if shopping gives you big thighs. I should ask a scientist. My dad's thighs are white and skinny. I do see big thighs on women shopping in town, but they are not muscly. I can tell because they wobble in a different way to muscle.

At first it was difficult to see what kind of skin the creatures had because I was far away. The legs were bare skin, like a reptile, no feathers or hair (like my mum's legs, sometimes). (Not that my mum's legs are 'reptilian'. In fact the creature's legs were nothing like my mum's.) Its body was a mixture of bare skin and fur or short feathers. It had a big body and smaller arms coming out from the front of its body. It had similar claws on its hands, but nothing as big and scary as the claws on its feet.

It was scary just the way it looked. I wondered to myself whether a big chicken would be as scary and decided that, although it would look weird to have a giant chicken in my garden, chickens don't have 'attitude' – another of my mum's favourite words. 'Don't you give me attitude, young man,' she would say. I wasn't giving her anything. I was just thinking – taking on board what she had been saying. Sometimes I don't know what she is talking about and it takes time to process things in my brain. Sometimes she will ask (no, in fact 'tell') me to do something and just because I have not figured out exactly what is the problem is, I have an 'attitude'. Sometimes I would just suggest that we vote on something believing it would be good way to decide what should be done. But no, apparently it's an 'attitude' to think like that. When people want to vote it's no wonder there is so much war around.

What is it with democracy? Why is democracy a good thing when it doesn't apply to children? They say children have human rights, but do we have to be protected *from* democracy? As if we're dangerous or something. Or democracy is dangerous. Which is it? What is the worst we could do? If a boy had a rubbish idea, nobody would vote for it. If it was a good idea, it might get lots of votes and then why would that be a bad idea? Grown-ups say we have to learn from experience. What they are really saying is that we have to live by *their* experience. If they really wanted us to learn by our own experience, then we should be allowed to vote. Then the grown-ups would have to argue using logic and facts. But that will be their weakness and they know it. It's a conspiracy of grown-ups, by grown-ups, for grown-ups.

So, I am glad there are creatures in the world like the one in my garden, because they scare grown-ups. Grown-ups know they can be eaten. Therefore creatures have a role in our society. So as I grow up myself I think I will always try and defend the rights of these dangerous creatures, because at the very least they are doing boys, like me, a service.

– VI –

Every year we have a parade in the town. Lots of people dress up and walk through the town including the mayor and town councillors, but I am getting a bit sick of it. The mayor is fat and the town councillors are getting fatter. The mayor always walks at the front waving and smiling. He must eat so much. He is leaving his job of major two years early this year. Health reasons, he said. I think he could just eat less. They say it is because he was embarrassed by the scandal of the eaten boy. After the creature had its meal, the mayor said lots of things about going out into the woods and hunting the creatures. He would 'lead the way', he said. When he was invited to actually 'lead the way' into the woods though, he suddenly didn't want to go and said it would be better for younger men to lead the way. So people told him to get out the way.

I will not be sorry to see him go. He wasn't much of a leader. It is always the politicians and wannabe leaders who talk themselves up. I think we should vote for the leaders from those people who do not put themselves forward. Ambition in an adult is a dangerous thing. Perhaps more dangerous than the creature in the garden. After all, how many people have been killed by someone in their role as a leader? If I found a mayor or any other politician in my garden I should be more worried. This made me feel better and less scared as I watched the politician, I mean creature, in the garden.

It had a thick, strong neck that did not slow its movement like a hippopotamus. It was similar to a horse's neck. At the end of its neck was a lizard-like head. A cross between a horse and a crocodile. There were no feathers or fur on its head, but there was brightly-coloured feathery fur running down its neck – blues, greens and some bright reds. It looked as if it knew what was going on around it. It was careful, but not scared. The eyes were steady and focused, then moved very suddenly to another part of the garden, but it was not a nervous movement. It was not panicking. It was hunting. I did not know if it could see me through the two sets of reinforced glass. I imagined I was just a small fuzzy shadow to the creature, so I stayed very still. I could see its nostrils getting bigger then smaller. I was sure it could not smell me. It would move one way towards the garage and lower its head to the bushes as if it was smelling the flowers. Then it moved to the fence on the other side of the garden. All the while it was moving down the grass towards me.

It looked fast. Even faster than Gary Murphy, but I couldn't prove it. I imagined Gary running down the garden from the wall to the conservatory followed by the creature. I think the creature's thighs would show who was boss. Gary might make it halfway, but not three-quarters. But then I thought if Gary knew he was being chased he might run faster and he might make it three-quarters down the garden. I imagined him running, being chased by the creatures. I feel bad because it made me laugh. He would be so scared, his eyes would be bulging out and he would be screaming as well. That would show him. Then I thought if Gary was screaming as he ran he wouldn't make it three-quarters of the way. Maybe not even halfway. But I imagined the first spurt of blood might reach the glass.

Before I knew it, the creature was ten feet away from the first set of reinforced glass of the outside conservatory. Now there was only the laundry wheel between the house and the creature. It stopped and was looking at the wheel. It probably didn't know what it was. I suppose it looked like a tree. As the creature took a step past the metal tree, its shoulder brushed the side of the wheel. I know it squeaks when it moves, but I couldn't hear it through the reinforced glass. The creature heard it though, because it stopped and looked puzzled at the revolving tree until the wheel stopped moving. It took a step, then another step brushing a spoke making the wheel move again. The creature then pushed a spoke with its nose making the metal wheel turn. Maybe it just wanted to play. One more step and turn. Now the creature was directly outside the conservatory glass, almost with its back to me. I was relaxed. It was playing. I leaned in for a closer look and put my hand on the inner glass door. That's when it changed. The creature suddenly turned. Its body hardly moved but its head and eyes swung round and looked directly towards me standing behind the glass. It had lost all interest in the laundry wheel.

I stood deadly still. I was confident that if I did not move, it would not see me. I have been playing in the garden many times and I know that when the sliding doors are closed the reflection from the daylight off the glass means a person cannot be seen in the house. If I could count the number of times I have been playing in the garden with the two conservatory doors shut (inner and outer) knowing that my dad or mum was keeping an eye on me, I would get really bored.

On two occasions I tested my mum and dad. Not that I test my parents in a bad way. I am not testing whether they love me, but I am testing their attentiveness. I think it keeps them on their toes which is good, not so much for me (because I am responsible), but there will come a time when my baby sister will want to play in the garden and my mum and dad will definitely want to keep an eye on her. Personally, I think she will be totally rubbish about keeping an eye out for creatures not only because she is a little girl, but because I have never seen a girl run as fast as a boy. I have seen some girls who can run pretty fast, but they are rubbish in other ways. It is difficult to run when you are screaming. Boys don't scream as a rule. Well, I don't. Never will. Not like Gary Murphy. (Although, technically, I had never seen him scream while he ran, so I accept that my argument isn't logical. Not yet.)

Anyway, the test. I was always told not to go beyond the windows of the garage (which is not even halfway down the length of the garden). I had just turned eleven and I was bored of playing near the washing whirligig metal tree. Both reinforced windows were closed. A creature had not been seen for at least three weeks by anyone, anywhere. So, I headed a bit further down the garden. I was about to reach the garage window when I heard my mother shout, 'don't let me come out there and get you'. I turned and looked and couldn't see past the reflection in the glass. So I was pretty sure the creature would not see me even though I was standing twelve feet away. (The conservatory is about ten feet deep.)

Now it was facing me directly. When the creature was in the middle of the garden it was looking in my direction with one eye only. This was because the eyes are on either side of its head, not both in front like us. So when it was standing there looking at me directly I was unsure that it could see me. Unhappily, I thought it could, because it was now not moving its head around. Its eyes were focused directly forwards. Nothing was distracting the creature. Then, it took a step towards the glass. Had it seen something? I had not moved. I was still standing dead still although everything else inside me was jumping about. Maybe the creature has special eyes and can see through reflections. Maybe it can see though the reflection of pools to see fish swimming underneath the surface. It might have eyes like that.

Then it took another step, this time off the grass and onto the concrete path in front of the conservatory. It was at this point that I could just hear the tap-tapping of its middle claw on the concrete path, as if it was drumming it fingers. (It must have been very loud if I could hear it through the reinforced glass.) Was it impatient with me? Had it seen me from the woods? Was it hunting me? Was this the creature that had killed the boy the year before? Descriptions of the killer-creature said it had been mostly black and a few golden yellow feathers on its neck and head and under its tummy.

Then one final step. Now it was directly outside the conservatory and the outer doors of reinforced glass. It was still not moving its head and not looking in any other direction. I could not understand it. Why was it was looking directly ahead? At me? After a while it slowly raised one of its claws and reached towards the glass door. Did it know what it was? It did not matter. It knew the glass was there because it started to tap the door testing it. Then it reached higher and with its sharp middle claw pushed into the glass. I thought the glass was impossible to crack, but the creature leaned its body into its claw-talon and I heard a pop that echoed around the conservatory. In less than a second cracks like lightening bolts shot in all directions. The creature paused before leaning in again and slowly using all its strength to drag its claw down the glass. Screeching cracking sounds (big and small) bounced around the conservatory.

It was incredible. Its talon cut into the reinforced glass leaving a deep scar. For a moment I thought the whole door would shatter. Then it raised its claw again and drew another longer cut down the glass. Then it dropped its foot. It leaned forward and sniffed the scars it had made. I still wasn't moving and believing the creature was losing interest, I began to relax. I felt that I hadn't breathed for such a long time and so I breathed in then sighed. I knew immediately that I had done something wrong. As my chest rose with air then sank as the air went out of me, the creature suddenly twitched its head to the side as if I was trying to get a better look through its left eye. It leaned forward towards the glass. I was totally focused on its eye looking straight at me, so when there was movement at the far end of the garden I didn't really notice. Nor did the creature, because it took a step back, raised its foot and its middle talon again. This time it didn't scratch a new cut in the glass, it placed its talon in the first cut of the glass and pulled it down cutting deeper into the glass door. Maybe it thought it was ice. It was trying to get through. Just as it finished this third scratch, it stopped, suddenly alert. I too was now aware that there was movement further down the garden. Without moving I somehow refocused my eyes to the moving objects at the bottom of the garden. It felt strange because it was the first time I had taken my eyes off the creature since its arrival in the garden. I don't think I had even blinked during the whole time.

– VII –

The creature saw them at the same time. Sam, Johnny and Nick were slowly creeping their way down the garden towards the creature. Sam was carrying a long thick stick, Johnny was holding a sickle and Nick was carrying a garden fork. Now I know Sam, Johnny and Nick were all bigger than me but they weren't proper men. They were eighteen and nineteen years old. Sam was the brother of a friend of the boy who had been killed the year before. Johnny was Sam's friend and was supposed to be joining the army. Nick was the son of the local shopkeeper. I didn't feel good about it and thought they would probably get eaten too. It might get really bloody. And I had a ringside seat!

Having a ringside seat had its problems, though. What was I going to tell their parents? The questions would come. Do I say I was sorry for their loss? How much time should I waste answering their questions? Or do I tell them what happened right away and describe all the blood? Mothers don't like hearing about that kind of thing even if their sons are grown-up. I didn't want to be in the middle of all that crying. Then I felt even more bad, because I didn't want there to be a fight not because I didn't want Sam, Johnny and Nick to be eaten, but because I didn't want to be surrounded by sobbing grown-ups asking me questions. As I thought this, I found myself wishing I was in the garden with Johnny, Nick and Sam.

Then I thought, what if they died and I survived? It would be even worse, so I decided to stay indoors for the time being. It is not as if the boys were trying to save anyone. I wasn't even in the garden, so the adults couldn't blame me and say: 'why were you in the garden when you knew it was dangerous? That is why the three boys jumped into the garden – to rescue you! How irresponsible!'

Therefore I was quietly hoping the creature would get scared and back up out of the garden and over the wall which wasn't that far away. But then the situation got worse. Just as I was thinking about the creature disappearing over the wall, I looked at the wall. And what did I see? More movement. It wasn't another boy coming into the garden to save me (even though I wasn't in the garden), no, it was another creature. And this creature was so much more scary. It was bigger and completely black. Black skin, black feathers and a black face. The only bits of colour were the golden feathers sticking up and running down its neck from its head to the body and the golden yellow of its eyes. I knew immediately that this was the creature that had killed the boy the year before.

Sam, Johnny and Nick hadn't seen the second creature. They were slowly approaching the first creature and trying to circle it, but the garden was too narrow which meant they all had their backs to the danger behind them. They were waving their weapons trying to scare it, but their waving wasn't scaring me so I doubt it was scaring the creature. The creature was not really reacting. For a moment I did think of opening the conservatory doors to let the boys run into the house but then Nick, who was edging along the fence, saw the second creature slowly walking down the garden towards them. Nick now had his back to the fence with the first creature to his left and the second to his right. I could see the boys shouting to each other and Nick obviously told Johnny to watch out because Johnny spun around to see the bigger, golden-feathered creature behind him. Waving the sickle didn't seem to help. The new creature kept approaching so when Johnny swung at the creature it nearly hit its black body but it wouldn't have mattered because the creature stepped forward raised its right claw, extended its middle talon and stabbed straight down into Johnny's chest pulling down and ripping open his body. It was incredible. Johnny's body just opened up and his red insides spilled out onto the grass. It only took a second. I didn't hear any screams and noises because the glass was just too thick, but I am sure there were a lot. Johnny was on the ground but it did not stop the creature clawing away at him opening up the massive gash. Soon Johnny was just a limp doll. I bet the others wished they had never jumped into the garden.

While all this was going on Sam was waving the stick up and down trying to get a clear hit to the head of the first creature. I don't want to do Sam down, but he was pretty rubbish. It was almost as if he was trying to play tig with the thing. Nick, still with his back to the fence, had a better chance with his garden fork. Although shorter than Sam's stick, it was sharper and would hurt the creature more if it connected. As things were becoming more serious and Johnny was meeting his death, Sam stepped forward to try and whack the first creature on the head, but this meant that the creature stepped backwards and into the Nick's pitchfork. Nick didn't even try to strike the creature, but the fork got the creature's attention and it span round quite angry. Throwing up its leg and catching the pitchfork head with its talon, it dragged the fork down to the ground. Stupidly Nick was still holding the long shaft of the pitchfork so found himself suddenly bent over and vulnerable to attack. Keeping the head of the pitchfork pinned on the ground with one claw, it raised its other claw high and brought it down onto the back of Nick's neck. The middle talon almost took Nick's head off in one swift movement. It was incredibly fast. I was impressed by both creatures' skills, but I suppose I shouldn't be surprised. Apparently they are millions and millions of years old and have become very good at what they do. Humans have only been around for a few tens of thousands of years. We have developed brains and different ways of fighting, but watching the events in my garden they were not very effective.

Finally there was Sam. He was now against two creatures both approaching him slowly. He didn't have a chance. It was difficult to say which creature attacked first. Maybe they had agreed a sign between them. It seemed as though they attacked at the same time. Sam almost fell down before he was hit, but I cannot be sure. This time they seemed to attack with bites. The claws were used to hold him down and when they went in with their teeth, I had to look away. This was the first time I turned away. I couldn't face it. I closed my eyes and breathed out. All the air seemed to leave me. It had all happened so quickly. Johnny and Nick were dead within seconds of each other. About five seconds after that, Sam had been jumped on by both creatures. I thought about the fat mayor. I didn't know whether he was clever not to lead people in a search for the creatures or if he was a total coward. It would be interesting to see what he had to say about the events in my garden. After this I couldn't see any mayor leading volunteers into battle. Mayors just seem to like jewellery and swords and walk around with their chests puffed out in front of crowds. Beware the fat politician, I say.

– VIII –

I did not want to watch anymore and started pacing back and forth thinking about what I should do. I was muttering to myself I think, but not very loud, so my muttering couldn't have disturbed the creatures. As I looked up and out towards the garden I saw both creatures standing very still over the body of Sam, their noses bloody, looking in my direction. Just like the first creature had done. I stood completely still and tried to slow my breathing, but it was impossible because the creatures were now moving towards the conservatory. Could they really see me? As they moved towards the conservatory, their heads did not move. The legs and the rest of the body did, but their heads seemed to glide at the top of their bodies. They did not look in different directions either. Just straight forward. At me.

They reached the conservatory and stopped, looking in. I did not move. I wondered if other people would come over the fence. If Sam, Johnny and Nick had known there were creatures in the garden, then others might know. Trouble was, because they were older, their mothers might not know where they were every minute of the day. Incredible though it sounds, they might be allowed to roam free like dangerous creatures or grown-ups. Nobody would notice them missing. It might give the creatures enough time to cut through the glass. My mother and sister were due back home soon, so they might also be attacked.

The bigger black creature leaned forward. Its nose touched the glass then pulled back. After a second it moved forward again and its nose pressed against the glass. It snorted in frustration and blew out lots of Sam's and Johnny's blood on the glass door. Mum wouldn't be pleased.

Then something disturbed it. Possibly a sound from the garden or the field. I don't know. I didn't hear anything. They both turned suddenly and lost interest in the glass and conservatory and trotted off back down the garden pausing by Nick's and Johnny's bodies for a last nibble. They bent down and stuck their mouths into Johnny eating his insides. He must have been tasty because it looked as if the creature was trying to gulp down the insides quite quickly. The first creature was eating the flesh of Nick's neck. It shook the body. It clawed at Nick's chest opening up his body and started to chomp on the red bloody mass. Biting and pulling at the flesh. Then it returned to the neck and bit and chewed some more. The final time Nick's head came off. The creature had eaten right through his neck. Nick head bounced and rolled into the flowerbed running along the fence of the neighbour's garden. I knew that would upset his mother. I might leave that detail out of the final description I thought, unless I was asked the question: 'what happened to my beautiful son's head?'

Then whatever disturbed them the first time seemed to happen again, because suddenly both creatures stood up and their eyes and heads started twitching. Then without taking another bite, they turned and trotted off towards the end of the garden. They never looked back in my direction. They reached the wall and within seconds both had disappeared. I would say that everything was now quiet, but during the whole event I had hardly heard a single thing. Everything looked quiet. I stood there looking at the view maybe for a minute or so. Three boys I knew lay around in pieces. They had been running around and alive only minutes before. Now, nothing. I suppose I should have run out of the front door on to the street and pulled the street alarm, but I was exhausted. Looking at dead people knocks you out.

I unlocked the inner door and slowly pulled it back afraid the noise might alert the creatures, but they didn't reappear at the wall. I took a few steps towards the outer door, carefully put my fingers on the lock release and was about to pull it back when I saw the print of the nostril and the blood spray made by the big creature. It was odd to think it was not the creature's blood, but from someone I knew. I looked again at the two scratches on the glass made by the first creature. One was certainly deeper that the other. I think the glass would have held. Turning my attention again to the garden, I saw it was empty of danger. I released the lock on the door and pulled it across. After a moment I stepped down on to the concrete path and then on to the grass. Everything was silent in my garden, but I heard a few doors slamming in gardens nearby and a few muffled shouts. With my eyes on the wall at the end of the garden I took ten paces forward and arrived at Nick's and

Sam's bodies. It was incredible. I spotted Nick's head in the flowerbed. I slowly walked over and picked it up. I thought people should find it close to his body. And besides, his mother would be here soon.

It was then that I heard the gasp and muffled scream from behind me. I turned and saw my own mother standing in the conservatory door with one hand over her mouth, her other hand over the eyes of my little sister pulled in close to her mother. It must have been an odd sight seeing her son standing in the garden holding the head of one of the neighbours surrounded by bodies and blood. She had only left me alone for twenty minutes. It didn't look good. How am I going to explain this, I thought. This is crazy.

'It wasn't me,' I said just in case there was any confusion about the facts. Although my mum knows that I am a responsible person and wouldn't do this kind of thing, she does like her logic, so I had to be careful. 'I can explain everything,' I continued. 'It has been a really scary afternoon.'

I took a deep breath.

'But I never screamed.'

The Florin Smile

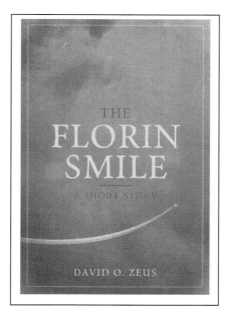

> *Borne on flaming chariots of rock, in the infancy of time*
> *A gift once came from heaven and earth became a home.*
> *Soon another gift will find its way, a further gift sublime*
> *And make this home a heaven; a heaven in our time.*
>
> Book of Berossus.

I. Before the Storm

Jennifer had always wanted to be in the business of caring. What better place to care than in prime-time television news – the 'biggest' in the business of care (and as a news anchor, no less). To sit in a chair, a place from which one could coordinate the caring of millions was humbling indeed. In fact, in her television-humble opinion (if that wasn't a contradiction in terms), broadcast news was the pinnacle of human achievement. It connected truth with service, service with power and people with her. She connected with them and they 'connected' with her. In fact the television news anchor herself was the pinnacle of human evolution (in her opinion). She cared and through the gift of technology (and her smile, of course) everybody knew it.

If a viewer didn't know any better he or she would think the beautifully turned out newsreader was selling something, toothpaste perhaps. She had lost count of the times she had been approached to appear in television commercials, but she was better than that, better than shampoo, better than toothpaste, better than any women's toiletries and, although she would never admit it to camera, better than weather forecasting. She could leave that kind of thing to Masha. Sure, Masha, was reasonable-looking in her way and viewers enjoyed her weather forecasts, but they would never believe Masha cared for them. Not like her. Jennifer was a step-up all areas: her role was to sit at the centre of the studio look directly into camera and, with her artfully developed warmth of manner, she would inform, reassure and brighten the living rooms of millions, all with lashings of sincerity that would melt the heart of a polar bear caught in the coldest of ice-ages.

So, it was a little ironic perhaps that the story she was about to introduce would change the world. Slowly, but surely. Not just her world, *the* world (they weren't interchangeable).

'Scientists have known for a few years now,' Jennifer announced solemnly to camera, 'that the gravitational pull of a family of comets that passed through the Kuiper Belt a hundred years ago dislodged a handful of deep-space objects which are now headed our way, but it is only now that we know that they will hit the earth later this month.'

Jennifer didn't fully understand words she was speaking. The words were written by another, but someone had to read the autocue and that 'someone' didn't need to write nor understand as long as she could read and care. Caring was her currency, after all.

'Have no fear,' Jennifer continued, 'the objects are no bigger than cars and will mostly burn up in our atmosphere falling only as dust if it makes land (or water). For the in-depth story, we turn to our science correspondent, Max.

'Tell us more, Max,' Jennifer said turning to her colleague with smile perfected first in beauty pageants then in media-training. A smile that, as the enthusiasm of youth receded would be replaced by the complacency and smugness known only to a chosen few. 'What's this all about? Should we be worried?'

'Firstly, Jennifer, can I say just how great you are looking this morning,' Max replied.

'Why, thank you Max. You too. Now tell us, is this the end of the world as we know it?'

'Well, no, Jennifer, we shouldn't be worried,' replied her colleague with an earnestness learnt in childhood studying televised studio chat. 'It is an interesting phenomenon though, a coming-together of a lot of interesting cosmic stuff. Using deep space spectrometers, the scientists have determined that the outer space objects are carrying a compound virtually unknown on earth called Selenium Tetraflorin-hexafloride 14.'

'Big words. Sounds crazy, Max.'

'Big words, and crazy indeed, Jennifer. It is believed this compound might have an effect on organic matter,' Max said nodding to his colleague, who responded on cue.

'Are you calling me organic matter?' she said pulling a face to camera as rehearsed.

'Well, not to put too fine a point on it, yes, you are,' Max replied before turning directly to camera himself and escalating the earnestness in his brow. 'Lab tests over the last ten years have suggested it could be an aphrodisiac for the brain.'

'Aphrodisiac?'

'For the brain, yes, it will possibly enhance neuron connectivity and serotonin generation.'

Jennifer glanced down at her script.

'Has this happened before, Max?'

'Well, yes, quite possibly. Geophysicists have discovered very thin layers of the compound in rock samples that correspond to astral showers every 160,000 years, the last being at a layer dating to 40,000 years BC.'

'So, this time it's early?' asked Jennifer.

'Yes, and what's more, the solar minimum will allow more ultraviolet UVB light to pass through the atmosphere and reach earth; this, the scientists think, will react with the alien compound with unknown consequences. Throw in the gravitational waves hitting us from deep space and the seismic activity we have been seeing which might disturb the deep-earth seas means we have a pretty exciting time ahead of us.'

'Deep-earth seas?'

'Don't worry Jennifer, it just means that the deep-earth seas caught 400 to 600 kilometres down between the upper and lower mantles will be forced up. It is believed the Selenium Tetraflorin-hexafloride 14 compound dissolves in water and in particular concentrations can impact organic matter in a way we have not seen for over forty thousand years. In short, if it rains down from the sky and bubbles up from the deep earth, we might have a few excited scientists bouncing around; this kind of compound is virtually impossible to manufacture in the laboratory.'

'It's the perfect storm.'

'The perfect storm.'

'Max, how will this effect us? People. Human beings. Me?'

'Well, if (and it's a big if) enough Selenium Tetraflorin-hexafloride 14 enters our ecosystems it might literally be an epoch-making event.'

'And we all become cleverer?'

'Nobody knows, Jennifer, but it is true, there are theories out there that these kinds of alignments correspond to significant changes in life on earth becoming a catalyst for brain development. The compound's arrival has coincided with the arrival of homo sapiens 200,000 years ago and the great human migrations of 40,000 years ago, so maybe we'll have our own jump in human development. Who knows.'

'I don't, Max, but thank you,' said Jennifer turning to camera. 'Don't worry folks, I think Masha can give us something to smile about. What's going on with the weather today, Masha?'

II. After the Fall

Jack didn't have a name when he fell, or rather nobody knew it and nobody cared in that street or any surrounding street. The shock of his tumble from his bicycle was beginning to wear off leaving his junior colleague's words (words that might in fact have thrown him off his cycling game) still echoing in his head. It had been the first time in his life that he had been referred to (albeit haltingly) as middle-aged. How could she do that? His waist band had grown no more that two inches than when he was at his record-breaking fittest as a student. Yes, he knew that the toned arms, shoulders and abdomen had been traded in for seniority (sitting at a larger desk) but he was in still far better shape that his contemporaries who did not cycle. As for the choice of cycling itself it showed a rare sense of daring on London streets, not to mention demonstrated a keen pragmatism. It was quicker and cheaper (both arguably not the tendencies of a 'middle-aged' man).

Angry and distracted as he was, her words might well have been the reason he had jostled with the black cab. The vehicle was going too fast and its driver probably thought he could overtake Jack ahead of the concrete pedestrian island in the middle of the road. But the cabbie couldn't and hadn't, and had swerved in. Jack had tried to maintain his line but his bike clipped the vehicle. He hit the road before he knew he had fallen. Had he been knocked out momentarily? He did not know. Once on the tarmac it was the sudden appearance of a large truck breaking to a stop and towering over him that had his attention.

As his shoulder ached, his head hurt and his hip stabbed with pain, he was aware that commuting frustrations and delays would ripple out from that side street. It was rush hour – a time when people got in the way of everybody else. Besides the cycling route to work was in a forest of roadworks – barriers, bollards, cones and zones were everywhere. It frustrated everybody and to such a degree that, in recent months, laws had come into force making it illegal for road-users (including cyclists) to move or circumvent any roadwork barriers, as had been practice. Prostrate, Jack cursed the law-makers.

The first horns were probably behind the lorry and snapped his mind back to reality, but his mind was far ahead of his body. He could hardly move. His body was frozen. Then there were the car horns behind the car horns. And so it was that the sounds began to ripple down the street. There was nothing he could do about it.

But then something extraordinary happened.

Recollecting events in the comfort of his home a few days later, he believed three thoughts had flashed through his mind.

First, that he was dying and she was an angel – the last gasp of his bruised brain in its de-oxygenated state before it malfunctioned altogether.

The second flash (which lasted a bit longer) was that he had *not* died and that the encounter with a smile, so bright and dazzling, was in fact life teasing him – either playing a cruel trick or providing a golden opportunity. Cruel in that, as he lay injured, an immobile, bloody mess, he was unable to invite the smile's owner to join him for coffee. Or, 'golden' in that a further encounter was assured because the possessor of such a smile would surely seek news of his recovery (and a coffee was on the cards being the least he could offer to his good Samaritan).

The third and final flash was that it didn't matter. Whatever happened, whether he lived or died, he had been witness to a blessed gift.

'Are you okay?' came the words from the light.

'Yeah,' he mumbled. 'I'd better move. I'm in the way.'

Like a symphony orchestra warming up, the street was now a cacophony of noise generated by the commuters in all directions. An ordinary London street had become a make-shift concert hall. Those not trapped in vehicles, rushed onwards to their destination with their eyes firmly fixed on the pavement in front of them, their conscience clear because one passer-by was in attendance (and two would be overkill).

'I'll go and talk to them, shut them up. Stay still.'

And with that, she and the light moved away towards the lorry.

Jack had heard the door of the lorry cab slam shut followed by a few heavy steps. A gruff voice barked a few recognisable words (something about a 'ducking cyclist and banker') but then it stopped. There was a pause, the light had moved in the gruff voice's direction. She spoke softly and before she moved further down the street he heard the tones of the gruff voice disappear as if dropped into a bowl of warm honey. A moment later the honey-sweetened voice of the lorry driver was by his side and soothing words were being showered over him while strong, stiff-fingered hands cradled his head.

'Don't worry about the others,' the gruff voice said, 'she's gone to have a word with them.'

And with that he heard the nearest horn die, then moments later the next until all the brass and percussion sections had fallen silent. Before long the players in the orchestra seemed to be around him offering soothing words of support. Those who weren't talking to him were introducing themselves to other members of the now-defunct orchestra. He could hear the smiles in their voices and the ever so gentle glow arise from the crowd. By the time the emergency services had arrived, it was a beach party – the sounds of people chatting to the gentle lapping sounds of a distant metropolis. Bizarre. Nobody thought they would be commuting to the beach that day.

As he was being loaded into the ambulance his observation was echoed by the paramedics.

'Apparently there was a girl here with one of those smiles.'

Yes, he thought, there most certainly was.

As he sat convalescing at home a few days later, he reflected on his time away from the office. He was indeed middle-aged, supposedly wiser, but some of that wisdom seemed to have been attributed in error. He was now conflicted. He had been trying to make a name for himself in his job, his life, the world at large and even his own head. Yet nobody had a name that day he was laid out on the tarmac. And it had not mattered.

III. Give! Give! Give!

'What is it?' Philippa asked her office colleague, concerned (not for his person but for his productivity).

'Oh, nothing,' George sighed and smiled.

'Did you sell it?' she asked, hoping to make the point that his current manner did not sit with the competitive nature of selling properties in Kensington.

'What, no,' he replied, impervious to her irritation.

'So what is there to smile about?'

'He's fallen in love,' Frank chipped in. Not that Frank knew, but he guessed. Frank had seen the shell-shocked George return to the estate agents immediately after the viewing with the client.

'No, it was just...right. The buyers can't afford it. But...,' muttered George, still distracted.

'But what?' Philippa asked.

'I am going to introduce them to the vendor tonight.'

'Them? The buyers?'

Philippa paused searching for the possible reasons for his attitude.

'Does one of them have the smile?' she asked, quietly.

George sighed and nodded. The jury was in, unanimous verdict.

'She does. Most certainly. And either her boyfriend is getting there or,' he shook his head and said, his voice trailing away, 'it's catching.'

'You know we work on commission, George?'

'I know but it is the right thing to do, Philippa.'

'Speaking as your team leader, I don't think the buyers should meet the vendor,' she said purposefully, trying to overcompensate for her own doubt. 'He'll just drop the price or come to some sort of rental arrangement. Both of which means you (and we) receive significantly less commission.'

'They can't afford it otherwise,' George protested meeting her eyes for the first time.

'Let them go to the mortgage provider and smile at them. Not the vendor. Then we have the best of both worlds.'

If George knew his team leader any better, Philippa thought, he might detect a lack of conviction in her voice. If Philippa knew her team any better, George thought, she would know he could see straight through her lame attempts at conviction. Besides, George had heard rumours that she had encountered the smile herself two months earlier at a family wedding.

The story went that in order to conduct two Saturday viewings of high-end properties Philippa had been desperate to decline an invitation to a cousin's wedding. To secure two sales that weekend would have considerably bumped up her monthly sales figures meaning she would smash her month's target, easily setting her on course to qualify her for a Level 2 performance bonus at the end of the year.

However, she had been frustrated at her family's insistence that she attend because she would have been the only family representative at the wedding owing to her siblings being overseas or hospitalised. After much stressful negotiation with the vendors and potential buyers she had managed to move the two jobs to the Sunday thus giving her time to race back to London to conduct the viewings. However, late on the Saturday, she had called her own boss begging (nay, insisting) he conducted the Sunday viewings himself because she was held up at the post-wedding festivities. The word in the office had been that she had smiled all the way through her boss's reprimand the following morning. It was a rumour that had been supported during that week by her exhibition of a rare calm – unbroken by the usual tear or tantrum. Why? It was learnt later that a guest at the christening had had 'the smile'. To what extent her encounter with the smile had affected her sales that month was unclear, but George estimated it would have contributed to a loss of many thousands of pounds of performance pay by the end of the year.

It was for this reason that George could see straight through his team leader's lack of conviction. A part of him half-expected her to insist on joining him on the pretext of helping him complete the sale, but looking at the lost look in her eyes George could see her thoughts had drifted back to the wedding. He suspected that Philippa feared that if she did indeed go along to his meeting (and encountered the smile for a second time) she would succumb once again and maybe even end up encouraging a greater reduction in the listed price. Such was the power of the smile, it could harm a business model. If they weren't careful their agency would end up facilitating sales of prime housing at affordable rates to the local population. It would be a disaster.

'They say it is in the water,' his colleague Frank said.

'I don't know,' George muttered rather wistfully. 'I'm not sure. We all drink the same water. The real thing comes from… I don't know. Elsewhere.'

Frank nodded and the three of them all looked over at the refreshment area. Where once a simple low-cost water tower had stood, now stood three – each holding a different 'water' from a different part of the planet. The costs of which were paid for by the staff directly.

'Why do you want three types of water?' the management had asked aghast when the request for 'alternative waters' was first submitted a month earlier.

'They each have different elements,' the team leaders had replied somewhat embarrassed.

'They are all one element,' the management had retorted. 'You'll be wanting a bucket of earth, a ball of fire and a bag of wind on the premises next.'

Learning that the management wouldn't be paying for it, the staff decided to purchase their different types of still water themselves – hard water from Norway, mineral water from Indonesia and glacial melt water from the Artic. It was ironic to see, a few weeks later, management also sampling the three types of water. Giving up on being surreptitious there was now open talk of ordering yet more water the Andean Patagonian forest region and even spring water from the Isles of Scilly. Rumours to the origin of the cause of the infamous smile had first surfaced on social media but were only now reaching the dinner parties of the well-to-do.

'Can I come?' Frank asked.

George and Philippa both looked at him.

'Tonight,' Frank continued. 'And meet her. I haven't met the genuine article.'

The young men both looked at their team leader inviting her to volunteer her own experience while framing it as seeking approval. She succumbed.

'I have,' she muttered, nodding. 'It is indeed striking.'

They both looked at her, waiting for more.

'It is a bit of a shock at first. Not so much the smile, but....'

The seated George nodded, still reflective. 'The peace?'

She nodded.

'The clarity,' she said wistfully before turning to George. 'You do realise the seller will probably just give it to them or give it at a price they can afford.'

'I know.'

'At probably one tenth the market value from six months ago,' Philippa added.

'I know,' George said, nodding.

'And you don't mind?' asked Frank, now bewildered.

'Well, you know. Whatever,' Philippa muttered as George shrugged.

'Why do they want to be in central London?' asked Frank

'She's been offered a job working on numeracy skills for children. She's on the minimum wage,' George mumbled.

'They'll up that,' Philippa mumbled similarly wistful.

'If I had the smile, it is the first thing I would do – ask for a raise,' said Frank looking at his distracted workmates.

The three of them knew it was not a viable thesis. The smile was a currency in itself. Why degrade it to pounds and pence?

'You know,' Philippa said furtively, 'this might be the third sale of a property at a massively reduced rate attributable to the smile.'

'I didn't know there were that many smiles in the borough?'

'There aren't. Apparently one sale went through because the vendor had encountered the smile the previous week on unrelated business, and the other two were buyers who had met people with the smile in the previous month.'

'And it had somehow rubbed off?'

'Who knows,' Philippa muttered, before adding, 'Some people have said I have changed.'

Finding themselves in difficult terrain, her two colleagues merely raised an eyebrow each.

'Er, what have been your sales this month?' George asked.

She nodded. Enough said. She knew she had indeed changed.

George paused. 'I've been thinking,' he said tentatively, 'of a new business model.'

He suspected his colleagues knew what was coming. He was about to speak the unspeakable.

'I'm thinking perhaps we should bring landlords together with people working in the area and looking for ways to provide affordable housing.

'The management would never go for it. The income would plummet,' said Frank shaking his head.

'But you are assuming that the landlord for our office premises,' Philippa said waving at the offices around her, 'cannot be brought onboard in the context of meeting with, say, George's buyers. We could still make enough of a margin to survive.'

George removed a document from his desk drawer.

'Just a draft. Want to have a look at it?' he said handing it to his team leader. 'Just five pages of notes. It needs work.'

IV. Take! Take! Take!

Apparently, gem stones nor precious metals were worth the risk. Neither was performing on the market. People with money were not putting it into the 'inanimates' as much. The market was saturated Danny had been told, and there was very little movement in the high street. So shifting stuff on the black market did not appeal to traders. Nevertheless, Danny thought the interest would bounce back. He would catch it on the upturn. So there was no harm in acquiring a bit of stock ahead of time. Treat it as an investment, he thought.

It was Danny's third proper job on his own, his sixth over all. On his first two jobs he had been given a five per cent cut, after which he managed to negotiate a ten per cent cut, but he felt he deserved more. After all he was putting his liberty on the line just as much as the other two. Even a 40-30-30 split would have been acceptable. Hence his idea to go it alone and find his own partner. But striking out on one's own had its dangers. Danny's own connections were limited and those he did know were moving on to other things, some retiring, some had been caught, others had lost their edge or heart (sometimes because of the 'happy' people they had met). He thought some of his old friends might be holding out for a larger cut, but no. So he had to find a rider with whom he had never worked. Jimmy hadn't risen to the top of the list from recommendations, rather availability on the day of the raid. It had to be a particular day and a particular time – so said the tipster. Having confirmed the details of the target premises from the tipster, Danny knew it was too good an opportunity to pass up.

That said, Danny wouldn't let Jimmy take fifty per cent. No, twenty per cent was more than enough, so he dropped it to ten. Jimmy had not been involved in any part of the planning and all he had to do was sit on the motorbike in the jeweller's shop entrance and remain ready to make the quick getaway. Danny would be the one inside doing all the talking (or rather shouting). The conventional wisdom had been that targeting an empty shop meant one is negotiating with the shop staff alone. However, there was a case for having shoppers present who might be carrying items of worth themselves. If not, the customers could act as leverage when he was negotiating with shop staff. Control the customers, you control the staff.

On this occasion the balance was just right, he concluded, as he stood in the middle of the swanky jewellers. They were a few staff and a handful of old codger customers. Danny felt confident and had been very persuasive. Collecting silver and valuables from the counters was swift. With business good he had not realised what was going on at the shop's entrance. For all his own continuous shouts of persuasion (coupled with the bike helmet he was wearing), he had not heard the motorbike's engine being turned off. There was a moment when he glanced over at the entrance and had seen a man talking to his partner, but Danny was confident that Jimmy would follow the agreed procedures when confronting meddling do-gooders.

As Danny's satchels filled with riches he found himself muttering thanks to the tip-off for the accurate information. A few hard cracks to the knees had dropped a few customers, some quite elderly, so they weren't going to get up and cause problems. Moreover, his aggression had hurried up the shop staff. He half-speculated that the staff were fearful of being sued by injured customers as a result of the slow transferral of merchandise. Customer Service at the high end of the high street rocks, he thought. Looking at the pensioners doubled up in pain on the ground clutching their knees, he didn't worry, it was not as if they ran, jumped, climbed or even needed their knees much any more.

Job done, Danny turned and raced towards the shop entrance to see Jimmy, his getaway rider, chatting with a man. Not only that, but a small crowd had gathered around the entrance and Jimmy.

'Okay, let's go,' he shouted through his helmet visor and punching Jimmy on the shoulder. Turning to Danny, Jimmy's expression, as seen through his own visor, looked quizzical.

'Hey, how ya doing?' Jimmy asked an incredulous Danny.

'What the ..., get a move on,' Danny shouted, pointing at the stationary motorbike, its engine off.

'You'd never guess who I just met,' Jimmy replied.

'I told you to keep the bike running,' Danny shouted.

'What?'

Communication is everything in the high drama moments of bank and jewellery heists, so it is ironic the perpetrators insist on wearing headgear that limits both the ability to speak clearly and be heard.

'I told you to keep the bike running,' Danny shouted, his voice muffled by the helmet.

'What?' repeated Jimmy again climbing off the bike and turning to him.

'Why did you turn off the bike? Let's go.'

'I was chatting to one of those guys. The bike was making a hell of a racket and I couldn't hear the guy. A really nice bloke. He asked what the problem was and what had brought me to robbery. I explained I had flunked school, lost motivation, had grown up without a father coz of a messy divorce. Anyway, this guy said he could help me. So this guy went off to get someone he had just met regarding a course for dyslexics – this smiling guy suspected that dyslexia was one of the things that was holding me back and these guys agreed,' Jimmy said, waving at the members of the gathered smiling crowd. 'They also said they would help if they could.'

'Get back on the damn bike,' Danny screamed through his visor.

'He told me not to go anywhere,' Jimmy protested, but seeing the Danny's glare through the visor, he gave in and climbed back onto the bike. 'Shoot. Ignition keys. Okay, where are they?' Jimmy said turning to the small crowd.

'They're behind you,' some cried in unison, laughing.

'Oh, you guys,' Jimmy said, shaking his head and playfully wagging a finger at the smiling crowd. Danny's heart, soul and stomach were plummeting. How had he been so blind to this moron? This was turning into a nightmare. Danny was now cursing the tipster who had proposed the target.

What Danny did not know was that the tipster, a bent cop, had manufactured this moment having had a rethink about his own policing responsibilities.

Some months earlier, the bent cop had been assigned to police a demonstration of some Middle East dignitaries on the very same day he had encountered the smile (in fact belonging to one of the polite protesters). As a result, and unusually for him, the bent cop had begun to reflect on his policing priorities and had learnt that the demonstrators were protesting against the protection by wealthy Arab business interests of a suspect in the murder of a young female Norwegian student. The murder suspect, the son of a Yemeni billionaire, had fled the murder scene (his London flat) and the U.K. in the hours following the murder. Given cause to reflect, the bent cop had dug into the background of the Yemeni suspect and had identified the jewellery store as being owned by his billionaire father. Hearing that robbery targets were being scouted by up-and-coming tough guys, the bent cop manufactured the scene and issued the tip-off to the unsuspecting Danny.

The cop had invited the protestor (with the special smile) to the coffee shop adjacent to the jewellery store at the designated time to discuss how the cop could be of assistance to the polite protestor's cause. Of course, the presence of a genuine, original smile attracted a crowd, but its attention was soon diverted to the sound of a revving motorcycle nearby. The smiler himself (and then others in the crowd) approached the dyslexic Jimmy. Having learned of Jimmy's back-story (freely shared by Jimmy), the man with the smile felt compelled to help the early-career criminal turn his life around. The Press arrived after a tip-off (from whom, no-one knew). And so, there they all were when Danny exited the store with all his swag and swagger and complaints about a quiet motorbike.

Before long, people were taking selfies with Jimmy and a confused Danny found himself handing out the jewellery to crowd members once the store staff seemed uninterested in taking it back when they too learned about the owner's connection to the prime suspect in a murder. After all, what were stones and little bits of metal compared to the life of a young woman? Before you could say Rumpelstiltskin, it was one big happy family, with everyone all smiles, mulling around on a non-descript street in the metropolis.

Of course, the Press had a field day. The murder was in the news again. Suddenly, the business interests of the suspect's billionaire father (and his ilk) collapsed as a result of social-media promoted boycotts. Not that it mattered, because the billionaire's remaining assets were frozen then seized, in part to fund the extradition request of the suspect. The Norwegian woman's family was grateful, the pensioners assaulted in the raid were more than pleased to participate in the campaign for justice. (They didn't run anymore, so no harm done.) The bent cop found himself smiling and endeavoured to uphold justice for as long as he had breath in his body.

Jimmy's educational opportunities materialised. Before long Danny was the only person in the room not smiling, until he too broke and sold his story to the Press.

Stuff was beginning to make sense. In common parlance the 'chicken or the egg' was replaced by 'justice or the smile'. In fact, the smile was beginning to reach deep into the criminal justice system and it was only a matter of time before the Martine's murderer was brought to book.

V. The Numbers

As the accountant, Mr Glaum, sat in front of his client in the client's lavish lodgings in central London, his overwhelming sense was that similar conversations were being held all over London that week. He was beginning to lose count of his own verbal exchanges with clients on the subject in recent months, but one thing had changed recently – the conversation was becoming increasingly tense. Normally lofty and composed tycoons were beginning to lose their cool. For decades these wealthy men and women had lived (and some worked) in a world in which they understood the currency of the planet and how to manipulate human behaviour, whether it be through the individual or the marketplace, to produce a financial return. Now, their understanding was rapidly becoming redundant. Why? Because their 'wealth', whether it be in stocks, share options, property, cash reserves or imminent inheritance, was plummeting in value. It could not 'buy' anything.

Ironically, Mr Glaum the accountant was quietly pleased that the phenomenon of the smile was being likened to a currency in itself – a way of trading and bartering. But it was trading that had no transferable value whatsoever to the US dollar, British pound, the Euro, the Yen, the Yuan. As a conventional 'currency' the smile did not have 'worth'. Yet, if the smile (or its unintended consequences) was becoming the way by which seven billion people interacted or 'did business', was that such a bad thing?

'I've heard enough of this fucking smile,' the irate, podgy man spat at the accountant opposite him as confusion and desperation dripped off his face. He paused. 'What is your fucking professional opinion?'

'Well, Mr Shaher,' muttered Mr Glaum before indulging in a moment of silence (a moment in which the image of the vexed tycoon clubbing a baby seal to death suddenly appeared in his mind).

'What?' the impatient man spat.

'I don't know how to say it,' the bespectacled accountant replied, before embarking on another moment of silence.

'Just say it, you fucking imbecile.'

A weak, embarrassed smile broke across the features of the accountant.

'You're not smiling,' Mr Glaum said a little sheepishly – a sheepishness borne of polite pity rather than deference. The foul language of the sixty-something businessman was rolling off the accountant's back. It was part of the background noise, like a litter around the litter bin – a shame, but not too much trouble.

'What? I am worth a fucking billion pounds!'

'Eighteen months ago, yes. Now, as I've said, it is pretty much twenty million pounds and falling. Give it a few months and...,' the accountant's voice trailed off. He waited for the litterbug to do his stuff, but nothing. Even the baby seals were safe. 'Your shares, any shares, are pretty much worthless now. Nobody is buying luxury items at exorbitant prices. The handful that do buy...luxury cars, for instance, end up sharing them.'

'And this fucking smile?'

'You mean the 'florin smile'?' the accountant interjected in all innocence. 'That's what they are calling it.'

'This fucking smile,' spat the billionaire finding his groove again. 'Have you seen one?'

'No,' the accountant lied, shaking his head in despair. He could never have predicted this conversation twelve months earlier.

'And how do I buy one of these fucking smiles?'

Mr Glaum smiled knowing full well that no one could buy the smile and the chubby tycoon opposite him knew it.

'How do I get one of these people with the smile to work for me then?'

'Well, that's just it. They're not for sale. Those in possession of this, er, particular charm, are not interested. Sadly.'

His last word was not heartfelt, merely an attempt to appear empathetic to the man who had spent forty years accumulating piles of a currency that served only to sit as data on a computer. That was what the world was all about up to twenty months ago – digital wealth. There was nothing to challenge it. But that was changing.

'I need to meet one of these people,' the tycoon hissed.

'They are out there,' the accountant replied gently nodding to the window whilst knowing that any owner of the infamous smile would be indifferent to the fat cat's wishes. And he himself was becoming increasingly sympathetic to such a view.

'So, introduce me.'

'I'm afraid I have no direct line to those blessed with the smile...'

Once upon a time the accountant would have kicked himself for using the word 'blessed' in such circumstances, but the little rebel in him was now pleased it had slipped out.

Perhaps his subconscious had slipped it into the sentence. How he wished to be in the company of such a smile right now. In fact, why should he be here at all? Why had he risen that morning, put on his tailored suit, endured the stomach rumblings only to sit and be on the receiving end of this colourful language that served only to drain him of his own colour?

He looked at the knotted face opposite him that had become increasingly strained and purple in recent months. If anybody needed to encounter the smile it was Mr Shaher. But how could he? The tycoon kept himself to his own tight social circles and was chauffeur-driven everywhere. No such man ever travelled on public transport – a practice that would increase the chance of an encounter with the smile (just as he, a lowly accountant, had experienced it quite suddenly one evening four months earlier at a distance of a dozen yards). He still found himself smiling when he thought of it. Its memory still warmed him one hundred and twenty-four days later. Remarkable.

Some tycoons, oligarchs and other well-to-do clients who were prone to try cosmetic surgery to possess a look not bestowed upon them by nature had paid for injections into the brain, into the face, into the stomach. They had had water flown in from every corner of the world. When alternative rumours as to the smile's origin had circulated, husbands and wives had locked themselves into freezing cabins at high altitude or insisted on weekly blood transfusions. No doubt some of the rumours that had swept social media were mischievous in nature. The so-called laughter clinics had had a bounce in popularity in the hope of attracting the smile virus (or toxin or whatever it was). When the source and cause of the smile proved elusive some of the desperate 'elite' tried a different tack. They lobbied for a change in the law saying such smiles were a threat to national security and a stable economy and that possessors of 'the curse' should be locked up. There was even talk of some business leaders suing those with the smile for loss of business. But how could a case be made against someone for 'unlawfully smiling'?

> *Your honour, the plaintiff contends that Ms X was smiling in the second week of July and was thus ultimately responsible for the loss of tens of millions of pounds of business and the company's subsequent collapse.*

Although one might argue that a smile might well have been responsible, no sooner would the 'defendant' be in the witness box, the jury, judge and all counsel would succumb to the smile and struggle to continue with court proceedings (and that was assuming the plaintiff could sustain his own anger). Or perhaps the defence counsel would demolish the argument by describing how those employees laid off from the company had in fact all gone on to find gainful employment in other companies (or even 'founded' companies themselves) or entered community-responsible work. And all such former employees would subsequently report a significant improvement in not only their own physical, emotional and psychological states but also those of their dependents. Consequently, the 'failure and collapse of the company' was not measurable by the employees' (from management to shop floor) well-being, but from the data listed on a spreadsheet in an oligarch's accounts. Arguably, therefore, the existence of the (now-defunct) company had had a 'net-negative' effect on the overall well-being of the country, so its demise should be regarded as a blessing.

Thus it was that Mr Glaum found himself almost pitying the man sitting in front of him. Mr Shaher was one of many who had lived in the belief that as one good fortune faded another would rise, but 'that fucking smile' (as his circle were wont to call it) had screwed everything up. The accountant pondered whether the definition and use of the term 'good fortune' in his own accountancy circles should be reconsidered. In his reflective moments (and as he witnessed the 'data-wealth' of his client-base diminish) he was beginning to think about seeking new clients. Not any old client. A new type. A smiler or those touched by the smile of others. He knew it to be ironic knowing they could not afford his rates, but, he noted, they probably did not have any need for his services. Even though he would offer them a good rate. Or rather whatever rate they could afford. Scratch that, a pro bono rate. In fact, were they short of funds and could he pay them a fee for his services? He had more than enough funds to see him through to the grave. You never know, it might put the fun back into accountancy. Accountancy might even become recognised as a 'vocation'.

One little secret Mr Glaum was keeping from his client sitting opposite him was that he had been invited to drop by a birthday party of an old friend that very evening. Normally he would not entertain such ideas, but there was a possibility that a florin smile would be in attendance – an acquaintance of the friend's daughter. In fact he suspected that his friend was having the birthday party in the hope that he would come face-to-face with the smile itself.

The smile that Mr Glaum had himself encountered, albeit fleetingly, when exiting a restaurant one busy lunchtime, had floored him. At the time they were quite rare. Not that they were common now, but it was still a little unusual to encounter one in the flesh. Approximately a third of his acquaintances had encountered a smile in person, but it was far from being a regular occurrence. There were reports they were on the rise, but some experts expected the number of people with the genuine florin smile would plateau. What was important, they argued, was not the number of smiles but the so-called ripple-effect on others people's smiles, attitudes and priorities – a perfectly acceptable by-product.

Nevertheless, Mr Glaum was a little nervous. If he did indeed meet a smile up close, what would be its effect on him? Would he buckle? Would he end up committing random acts of so-called kindness which, in his right mind, he would not even dream of doing (unless appropriate remuneration was involved)? Although he was not the panicky type and ridiculed the protests of many who saw the smile as a 'cancer on modern society', he was secretly conflicted. Perhaps he would risk it and pay a quick visit to the party. Just to see. What could be the harm? Besides, he might learn something and it might be fun.

VI. Nosebrase Lane

It was the day the irony chicken came home to roost, Jane concluded. It all centred around the street which was narrow enough to be closed to traffic – a favourite with lunchtime strollers (herself included) as it linked her office building with a part of town (the covered market) with the better sandwich shops. Unfortunately, this was a fact not lost on the homeless. Or rather one homeless man in particular. (As is common with homeless men he had no name, but for the purposes of this passage, we'll call him 'Ned'.)

So it was that walking down Nosebrase Lane had become a quandary for some office-workers – they could either take a quiet lunchtime stroll along the lane experiencing one minor annoyance (homeless man Ned) or a take a circuitous route along crowded streets to the covered market (and sandwich nirvana). It was a daily gamble. The circuitous route meant a rushed sandwich experience rather than the preferred leisurely break. That said, when it was raining, Jane felt sympathy for the homeless man. After all, maybe he had unwittingly fought in a war and was now paying the price for the trauma endured (while his political masters now consulted internationally for a fat fee). But there were other times (when the sun was out and the day's warm breath weaved its way down the lane) that she envied him – to be able to lean up against the wall all day, chilling out without a care in the world.

Nosebrase Lane was long and the homeless man's chosen position in the lane was closer to the far end (near the market), so she had enough time to adjust her walking pace to ensure that pedestrians entering the other end of the lane would be passing him as she herself was passing him. In the flurry of strides, everybody was ignored lessening the embarrassment for all.

On this particular chilly lunchtime Jane was delighted to see a number of pedestrians entering the far end of the lane (one hundred and fifty yards away) at a different time intervals. She was spoilt for choice. Leading the way was a fifty-something woman who actually stopped at the Ned's cardboard mat, bent down and chatted with him. Assuming the woman chatted for long enough, Jane surmised, it would be the best of all worlds – he received attention and she could walk by at peace, undisturbed. But then something peculiar happened. The homeless man removed the scarf from his neck and offered it to the fifty-something woman who duly accepted and wrapped it around her own neck. Audacious, Jane thought. The scarf woman and homeless man talked for a few more moments until the second group of young pedestrians caught up with the middle-aged scarf woman. Within a moment they were all talking. Gentle laughter was carried down the lane on a light breeze towards Jane who had slowed her walking pace unsure of the protocol now that the laws of the natural world seemed to have been violated. Would she somehow be dragged into the throng or was this indeed the best of worlds and she would slip by unnoticed?

She needed have worried. The homeless man rose to his feet and walked out the far end of the lane in the company of the other pedestrians. Whatever he had said must have been funny for they were laughing and smiling. The fifty-something scarf woman did not exit Nosebrase Lane with them. In fact she had continued on her way down the lane towards Jane. As they passed each other Jane kept her head down wishing to avoid contact but focused her gaze forward at the pavement. However, as the woman approached, the sun seemed to break through the clouds and a calm breeze swept down the lane prompting the birds to break into song. Thus, at the very last moment, and sensing she was missing something (a presence, perhaps?), Jane glanced at the woman as they passed catching sight of her profile.

Oh my god, Jane thought. The scarf-woman had the smile. Didn't she? Surely? Surely, not?

The novelty of working on a picture-desk at a national publication had long since worn off. Jane had only taken the job a few years earlier to support her life as an (aspiring) actress. The acting hadn't really materialised and, without so much as a warning, her life could be now measured in years rather than experiences; there was something about her day that had to be endured, rather than enjoyed.

What was interesting was that in her role working on the picture-desk she had witnessed at close quarters the impact of the smile in the media and in the public sphere. Once upon a time she had been one of the first people to see the pictures that would be break across the news networks in the following hours or days. A number of major scoops had come across her desk. The arrival of camera phones and social media networks had accelerated the process. Pictures could come from any luckily-placed citizen. It had its plus points when filling the pages, but it also meant that potentially newsworthy images flew around the world courtesy of chat and photo applications on the mobile devices rather than via the national publications or broadcasters. In order to compete, some publications had employed more dubious techniques to acquire more salacious or exclusive pictures. This had worked up until fifteen months ago but Jane was not the only one to notice that things had changed since the first smiles were reported.

Pictures of the bearers of such smiles had been sought by hungry editors. A few had come in, but the smiles were not captured convincingly and, as some said, it was apparent you 'had to be there'. The editors had pushed for more and better quality photos to capture the phenomenon in all its glory. Paparazzi had been dispatched. One or two photos had been published, but for some reason the newspaper circulation fell on publication. Word on social media was that people were not impressed by a newspaper's attempts to exploit what was essentially a good thing. The paparazzi were losing heart and even becoming sympathetic to the call for more respect. Engineers in the large multinational producers of image-capturing technology were puzzled over why the technology and lenses were not capturing the smile in its full technicolour glory. The phrase 'the camera never lies' had been turned on its head: 'the camera never tells' became the moan of editors.

So, in that momentary encounter in Nosebrase Lane, Jane never felt the inclination to pull out her camera phone and finally, truly understood the reports that other witnesses never had the inclination to do so themselves. Who, after all, pulls out their camera to take a picture of the sun? And what would it capture anyway?

After the encounter with the scarfed-woman's smile Jane had not seen Ned the homeless man for a week or so. She speculated that she wouldn't have minded had they met in the shadow of that woman's smile, but it was not to be. But after a few weeks, the gloominess of the lunch hour returned and she was grateful the homeless man had vacated her world.

But then, on this particular irony chicken day, she found herself walking along Nosebrase Lane minding her own business only to see him, Ned, slumped right up in the corner of the wall in his usual place. No pedestrians were in the immediate vicinity and Jane realised she would be upon him in moments. There was a group of people loitering at the far end of the lane but they gave no indication of moving. A stationary group of pedestrians – was there ever such a thing!

Jane shifted a glance from the homeless man (now two dozen yards ahead of her) to the group of pedestrians, who, with great relief, had started to move down the lane towards her and Ned. Jane adjusted her speed in the hope that by the time she reached Ned, they would also be upon them.

However, horror of horrors, Jane's glance at the homeless man revealed that he had seen her and was shifting in his position to accommodate her arrival. The drama was compounded by the slowing of the group of pedestrians. Was it almost on purpose? Before she knew it she was upon Ned and, succumbing to the weight of more horror of horrors, he was holding out his hand towards her.

Jane stopped. She manfully avoided eye contact as Ned struggled to his feet then took a few steps towards her, still holding out his hand and even waving his other hand at her.

And then, it was over. He, the homeless man, Ned, was beside her holding out his hand.

'For you,' he gasped, somewhat out of breath. 'I've been meaning to catch you.'

'What?' she blurted out, aghast and in disbelief at being acknowledged.

'For you,' he repeated with a part-toothless smile, still holding out his hand in which was a delicately wrapped piece of tissue paper.

'Marjorie gave it to me,' he continued. 'She suggested I hand it on to someone I thought needed it.'

He carefully opened the tissue paper to reveal a silver necklace with a finely-wrought star and bird attached as an adornment. Confess, she didn't, but it was really quite, quite beautiful.

'Initially I was going to give it to someone who had helped me, but that didn't feel right,' he said, still smiling. 'Seems silly to give something to someone who already has everything they need.'

Jane was stunned and hoped beyond hope that this was all a horrible case of mistaken identity and he, the homeless man, would come to his senses in a moment. He probably hadn't had his eyes tested for years.

'Apparently, it was a gift from a bride-to-be in 1900. I had it checked out with a local jewellers. It has history.'

'Why me?' Jane whispered.

'You passed me most days. You seemed unhappy to see me. I thought we would clear the air. Giving and receiving is a circle. You weren't giving so I guessed that you weren't receiving much either.'

'Oh, I've been receiving loads, thank you very much,' she replied indignantly.

'Apologies,' he said, 'you could have fooled me,' he added with a wink.

Jane didn't know what to say, so Ned continued.

'A group of us are gathering on Thursday after work, if you fancy joining us. It would be nice to know who we keep passing every day. Marjorie might be there.'

'Who's Marjorie?'

'A nice lady. A lovely smile. Has lots of friends.'

'And, er, who are you?' asked Jane.

'Eric,' the homeless man Ned replied, extending a hand. 'Don't worry, washed this morning. I regularly use that handwash stuff now. Only 69p from Superdrug.'

'Where did Marjorie get it from?'

'From a jewellers who thought Marjorie could do something useful with it. She swapped it for my scarf. She was looking a bit chilly. You can return it to the jewellers if you wish or get him to tell you the full story. Apparently they are giving away quite a few things. No point in keeping something that someone else might enjoy that little bit more, eh?'

She was trying to fathom out who the holy hell Ned-Eric was and what the holy hell was happening.

'And er …. what do you do?' she muttered.

'Oh, I just sit here and get cold. Watch the world go by. Much like you, I suppose, except you walk, not sit. So I suppose you pass the world by, rather than the world passing you by,' he chuckled.

She didn't know whether to be impressed or offended.

'I suppose the world passes us by however slow or fast we move,' he continued reflectively. 'But I'm at a stage of life when I'm slow enough that I should move around more.'

'Oh?' she said, still confused and wondering when this would end.

'I was very mobile once upon a time. I saw a lot of the world – for eleven years through a gun-sight. Trouble is, it gives you a bit of a skewed view of one's place on this earth. I struggled to focus on my return and could not focus on the here-and-now. I suspect you are at a point in your life when you're going so fast you ought to slow down. I think the trick is, move at the right pace as the 'here-and-now'.'

'Okaay,' she said, thinking this might in fact be the end.

'And you? Where are you going?' he said.

'It's my lunch break. I go to lunch,' she said nodding in the direction of the far end of the lane and towards the covered market.

'Always out to lunch?' he chortled. 'Well, I hope you have good company.'

'Well, sometimes it is nice to have some time to oneself.'

'What?' Eric said, playfully indignant. 'No harm in picking up a few new companions.'

Jane smiled, afraid.

'Why don't we get something?' he said. 'Don't worry. I've eaten. Hearty breakfast and you might not want to listen to my old stories, but I can introduce you to a handful of others,' he said nodding down the lane at the waiting crowd. 'In fact, truth be told, we've been waiting for you.'

Jane looked down the lane somewhat struck to see a crowd of half-a-dozen others whereupon they all waved at her and beckoned her towards them.

'Some of them work in an office too, so you might have something in common,' Eric said as they started to move. 'There Sylvie, Jemima, Geoff, a former postman and motorbike enthusiast..... .'

VII. The Seat of Power

Marie-Ann had never thought of herself as a victim. She had always been positive, but in the first forty-eight years of her life, she had felt she did not possess the currency to progress in her life, therefore she was obliged (even required) to serve those who did. The trouble was, those who did 'progress', (using whatever currency with which they were blessed) were essentially self-interested. The florin smile had changed all that. The door had opened and the light had shone through.

When she reflected upon what life had been like three years earlier, Marie-Ann could hardly believe people's ignorance. The world had reached a point where if 'heaven' were to be created on earth then a gift from the heavens was required. It had been beyond the wit of man alone to evolve.

Everything was being reassessed including assumptions dating back to the Garden of Eden. People were arguing the smile had been inherent in the biology of ancient peoples and a so-called 'fig leaf of knowledge' had covered up the truth. Social scientists were calling the last forty thousand years the 'Epoch of Adam'. A time of knowledge, a time of ignorance. It was catching on – the idea was sticking. Ignorance was acquired, not inherent.

And here she was, standing to attention in the corridor of 10 Downing Street along with all the other domestic staff waiting for the new Prime Minister to enter through the door. The hubbub on the street outside was being relayed on the television pinned high on the wall above her. It was her third time witnessing a changeover of PM. The first time she had been excited but a few years of working on the premises and seeing how government worked had left her jaded (or was it enlightened?). On the second occasion there had also been some hope before it all continued on its downward trajectory.

This time would be different, because the election had been won by a total landslide. Everybody had known what was going to happen. There were reports that the relatively insignificant proportion of voters who had voted against the winner had done so in order to deliver an 'Opposition' with which the government of the day could work in a constitutional setting. It would mean the Opposition would have to step up to the plate and would raise everybody's game for the next election in five years' time.

In the meantime, things were getting better already. Marie-Ann's own sister, Kit, had been blessed by the florin smile. She had first suspected during a phone call with Kit late one Thursday afternoon. Marie-Ann's sister had always had a pleasant, cheerful disposition and approached any obstacle as being part of life's rich tapestry. There had always been a smile in Kit's voice, but there was something else coming down the telephone line that day.

After exchanging hellos, Marie-Ann thought it might have something to do with the telephone line and thought nothing of it until she heard footsteps approaching Kit. The footsteps slowed before breathless, polite hellos were offered to Kit. The steps then moved off at a much slower pace. Sometimes the departing footsteps stopped as if the passers-by had stopped to look back. All the while Marie-Ann's sister was politely acknowledging hellos and thanking strangers in whose own voices Marie-Ann thought she could detect reflected smiles.

When the sisters eventually met, there was a change and no change. It was as if Kit had swallowed something. It was her sister, but there was a luminescence when she smiled. Marie-Ann subsequently learnt that a face required only five muscles to smile (as opposed to a frown which required fourteen), but it seemed as if those five muscles were connected to a different, highly-attuned, beautifully-oiled engine powered by some alien energy source.

Marie-Ann had therefore been privileged to see the effect of the smile in different environments – the domestic and political.

Marie-Ann had been able to purchase a small flat in Westminster meaning her commute to work had dropped to a ten minute walk rather than the one and a half hour commute. It had been the same for so many others. In the previous twelve months rent and property prices in London had adjusted (fallen) dramatically. Landlords and sellers were happy to help buyers with limited incomes. Though property values were worth a fraction of what they had been, there was no discernible damage to the well-being and living standards of the landlords and sellers. As a result of the trend people were moving closer to their workplace, commuting times plummeted and the city's congestion virtually disappeared (reducing commuting times yet further).

All of this had led to fewer irate commuters and more considerate motorists that in turn had led to more people cycling (their shorter journey to work). More road space had meant the buses had not been caught in jams, there was even talk of reintroducing trams for certain routes. People were sharing cars. The incoming government was keen to support these changes in law and limit the strain on individuals. The reduced commuting times and stress had meant workers were spending more time with their families or engaged in extra-curricular activities (sports, arts, hobbies). Relationships were therefore being kept in a better state of repair. A spirit of community cohesion was developing because people now had the time, the energy and the funds to improve the local areas. Crime was falling because there was less financial strain and more empathy with the dispossessed (supported by the aforementioned greater community engagement). Smilers were also volunteering in prisons which appeared to dramatically reduce re-offending rates.

Speaking of crime and criminals, the banks had to work harder for custom. There was less financial strife experienced by the average customer who was accumulating less debt. Banks accounts were flush with funds so banks were in the black and therefore more likely to lend to small and medium-sized businesses. Subsequently, interest rates on saver accounts were more competitive giving a better return. Disputes were solved more readily because banks and other retail outlets did not want to jeopardize good customer relations. In fact banks were moving away from a dependence on impersonal electronic banking because customers appreciated a face-to-face service. High street bank staff were encouraged to 'see the person behind the current account'. The experience and satisfaction of customers came ahead of almost everything else. Of course, this improved employment numbers in the industry and other industries followed suit feeding into the 'florin cycle' as people had started to call it.

There was less insecurity around the average person, less needless purchasing of goods as social interaction developed. Material goods became less of a factor in a 'having a good time'. A happier public was a healthier public. More time found its way into helping the neighbour, then the neighbour next-door-but-one, then the lady down the street and then the elderly chap around the corner. The strain on hospital Accident and Emergency services lessened. There was more time and support for convalescence in the community. Less work meant fewer long-shifts for the workers and, as Marie-Ann and commentators noted, all of this was complemented by the aforementioned shorter commutes, improved familial relationships and better financial returns on savings.

The developing feel-good factor was often based around the smilers who found themselves at the centre of many things. They were celebrated for their smile, for their attitude. They had incidental celebrity rather than the sad, needy celebrities of the Epoch of Adam. Smilers were not driven by ambition, plagued by insecurity. They did not appear on magazine covers, nor on television shows. They had better things to do. Smiling at a camera lens didn't give them a buzz any more that smiling into a lavatory bowl. Furthermore, those individuals who had once seen 'value' in spending their time in front of a camera lens lost any appeal to the public. 'Celebrities' could not offer anything of worth. In a toss up between spotlight or sunlight there was no argument. Their currency had been spent. Celebrities were a spent force.

Marie-Ann watched the Prime Minister's arrival at the door of the residence on a television screen that could never do justice to the wonder of the smile. Technology was losing its lustre. That said, a viewer could clearly determine whether an individual had the gift, but seeing it in the flesh (or any smile in fact) was what it was all about.

'This is the first time in a democracy when the leader of a country has not put himself forward for election,' the commentator said reporting on the televised events in Downing Street outside.

'And, it looks as if he will be the only one with a genuine smile in the Government, Eamonn,' one commentator said to another.

'That's more than enough. Besides, I think it might rub off on some of his cabinet colleagues,' replied Eamonn.

'Let's hope so.'

'The early indicators are that he has in fact appointed ministers who are experienced and even qualified to run their departments.'

'Fantastic, yes, Harry Manham, Edward Slab, Davina Bandil, all senior figures, have been omitted from the line-up.'

'The career politician has had his or her day.'

Marie-Ann had watched the outgoing Prime Minister's attempts to accommodate the changing political scene caused by the advent of the smile. Developing government policy to meet the changing times was a challenge, but identifying the politician from within the political ranks to take it forward had proved impossible. In time it had become clear: there was not a parliamentary political answer to the problem. The problem was compounded by the fact that no smiler had been (nor wished to be elected) to Parliament. The inclusion of a smiler had been explored by agencies and headhunters, but it was the exploitation of an old parliamentary rule that the Prime Minister did not have to be an elected politician that eventually won the day. The Prime Minister could run the government as a member of the House of Lords. No party wanted to be left behind, so both parties endorsed a leader from outside their ranks to lead an interim coalition. Changes in how the government did business were already being discussed including one in which policies were assessed against the 'Smile Index'.

Lost in her own thoughts Marie-Ann was suddenly jolted to her senses by the sudden rise in volume of noise. The thunder of camera shutters and shouting coming from the television's speaker was suddenly amplified as the door to 10 Downing Street opened. The noise flooded the reception hall and the interiors of the residence became at one with the outside world. In stepped the new Prime Minister followed by a few aides and the door closed. When the heavy bomb-poof door usually closed the reception room would drop into a heavy Victorian darkness. Not this time. Surprised by her own surprise she noted that when the door closed the corridor in which the domestic staff were lined up actually brightened. She had thought that her experience with her sister would brace her for the impact of the smile and give her a head start on her colleagues, some of whom had never seen it in the flesh. But no, as he approached the welcoming line, she knew she was as vulnerable and as pleased as everyone else.

Was this the end of a few weird years? Of, albeit welcome, topsy-turvyness? Or was it the beginning? Had the previous few years been a prelude to the real change? Looking at the Prime Minister's face as he moved down the welcoming line of domestic staff, she knew a return to the old ways was inconceivable, because the smile had found a home. Its own home. And it was heaven.

She glanced up at the television screen that had moved back to presenters in the television studio. Not everybody had 'the' smile, but some had echoes of it. Did an 'echo' of a florin smile count as a true smile? Or just a reflection of the genuine article? The television anchorwoman certainly had the echo. Marie-Ann was sure the technology could not cope with the real thing. It was probably blow the cathode ray tubes or TFT panels or whatever they were called. No, the newsreader, Masha, had the right smile for television. She was nice. She had been a weather presenter only the year before. And it was nice of the television station to keep on the payroll the old presenter, Jennifer, rather than kicking her out on to the street. After all, that didn't happen so much nowadays. Jennifer was okay, she had something of the old 'smug collective' about her perhaps, but it served as a reminder of a world gone by. No, Jennifer wasn't the real thing, but you don't need the real thing when presenting the weather.

Parked in a Ditch

I. A Plan

He was somewhere in middle-management. She was in the secretarial team. He was single, over one whole decade older than her (even closer to two small ones), in reasonable physical shape and of sound mind. She was in her mid-twenties with hair (long and brown). He had hair (some and brown). On his purchase of fashionable, thick-rimmed spectacles, colleagues likened him to the comedian Eric Morecambe (without the jokes). He had gleaned somewhere that she might have a boyfriend – the degree of 'seriousness' of which, he was unsure. He had noted her charms over the two-and-a-bit years they had worked in the same organisation. They interacted at regular intervals and engaged in cheerful chat whilst always maintaining their professional relationship. There was no flirtation and he had never targeted her for banter. It would have been inappropriate for him to engage in such things (or so modern society preached, he noted with sadness). Thus was he left gasping in the twenty-first century office.

He had had a 'busy-headed' few years, but the troubles had subsided and he was beginning to think of lighter, warmer things. Quite by chance (sort of), he was moved into a shared-office arrangement with the secretarial team. The boss had thought that he should become more closely involved in the work in which she herself was involved, which prompted thoughts to turn over in his head. Not that he was looking to get involved with her, but by being acquainted with the work in which she was involved, then maybe the grounding for them to become further acquainted might be laid (ultimately leading to something more than acquaintances....at a later date, in due course, possibly). Thus his thoughts turned and turned. It was progress, anyway – sharing an office. Besides, there was no rush. She wasn't going anywhere.

'I'm leaving,' she cheerfully announced one morning two weeks into Operation Bliss. 'Will you be my referee? Please?' she asked him.

He was happy for her. He did not have to hide his anguish because (it would be noted by neutral observers) a team-player leaving a team was a cause for anguish for everyone. Sobbing inside, he laughed and wondered aloud about the effectiveness of any job reference he might write – after all it might result in them sharing an office with each other for many more years to come, he joked.

Sadly, the prospect of any prospects with her seemed to lessen in the days following the news. One step forward two steps back, he thought. That's life. No sooner had he been promised a little bit of the promised life, a curtain is pulled back to reveal the slop. Laughter all around.

On reflection her proposed departure did elevate the matter and pose a question. A question that could be answered with careful planning for it presented a timeline in which something could be done. Must be done. His hand had been forced.

He could raise the matter during her last week, so there was no prolonged difficulty should things go awry. It would provide closure for him and an anecdote for her. And so it was that the matter began to play upon his mind.

It was not long before a plan presented itself. A large residential conference in a stately home out of town was scheduled to occur two weeks before her departure. The conference would be the ideal place at which to address the matter, far better than stumbling through a routine during office hours (and on office premises) all of which was laced with danger. Over the next two weeks 'a plan' slowly emerged in his head like meat through a rusty mincer. He would not be looking for an immediate result as such, just making a play for future consideration. Issuing an open invitation. Parking a thought in her head. Sowing a seed.

The conference sessions were scheduled to start on a Friday afternoon followed by a formal dinner in the evening. The Saturday would be busy with plenary sessions and breakout groups and the day would close with a second formal dinner. Sunday morning's conference timetable included a few more sessions followed by lunch after which the conference delegates departed.

His planning soon focused on the Saturday afternoon. He surmised that while the delegates were busy in their sessions, he would suggest that he and she retire to a side room to sit on an antique chaise longe and run through matters relating to her departure two weeks later. Being the senior administrator on site he would dispatch the third conference staffer to attend to conference business. Knowing that this third team member was stuck in a plenary session would allow him and her a gentle hour of quiet conversation. As discussion of her departure drew to a close he would casually work into the conversation his admiration for her making sure she didn't feel completely ambushed. It wasn't perfect, but it was a plan; a plan that could not be executed in the normal office environment.

As for the chat itself, it would be along the lines of an open invitation to meet up (with him) for coffee, tea, lunch, dinner or 'whatever' after she had moved to the new job and they were no longer co-workers. She would thank him. His careful delivery, warm but deliberate looks into her eyes, sideways glances at furniture items around the room (not to mention faraway looks at the landscaped gardens outside) would ensure that this was not some ordinary, run-of-the-mill invitation to a departing colleague to 'keep in touch'. No, it was a special invitation that was cleverly constructed so as to not permit an outright refusal. It was an *open* invitation after all. Invite her to dinner on Tuesday and she could turn it down out of panic and bewilderment. Inviting her to dinner on any Tuesday (in fact any day she chose) did not require an acceptance or refusal. Now that was a plan. He noted that once she understood that it was no ordinary discussion, she might clam up. This was to be expected, but knowing her as he did, he was confident she wouldn't crumble. Nevertheless, there might be confusion. Therefore it was important that he explained his thinking. It would broadly go as follows.

He liked her. He wanted to explain why.

He had reached an age at which he knew what he liked in a lady. He wanted someone who was cool and relaxed in her own skin, for, he believed, such a person would have a soothing affect on him. He would reassure her that she was not someone who was soothing to the point of being as dull as a doormat; she was, after all, stimulating company. It was important, he would explain, to find someone who could stretch him in ways he needed to be stretched. It was a tricky balance and she had the balance just right as far as he could tell and all wrapped up in a nice package, easy on the eye.

He wasn't stupid. He knew he couldn't use words such as 'doormat' or 'dull', but he would phrase it in a suitably appropriate way. He wasn't going to write down the words beforehand as had been his practice in his youth, no, he would play it by ear and pull on his years of experience in middle management. He hadn't got to where he was without thinking on his feet in numerous meetings. So, ironically, the plan was to lessen the planning.

He would remind her of his challenging few years explaining that he now valued the warm things in life, ergo her. The advantages of referring to his past were twofold. Firstly, he would be demonstrating a certain vulnerability and, secondly, it would deflect an adverse reaction should one be forthcoming. One phrase he had decided to include was 'don't beat me up'. He would spontaneously drop the phrase into the conversation at a carefully considered moment.

All he really wanted to do was plant a seed. He wasn't expecting anything at the conference. He expected her to sit there quietly, internally adjusting to the situation – from one in which her middle-management colleague sitting opposite her was advising her on filing to one in which her middle-management colleague was gently revealing that he was holding a candle for her. He knew that she knew him and that it should not be too awkward. There was no intention of putting her on the spot. He would end the conversation with the words, 'no rush, have a think,' and suggesting that if she fancied meeting up, even months later, the invitation stood. It was an *open* invitation. He even thought about miming the placing of an invitation on the coffee table and there it would remain for her consideration. However, if the gods so intended, the invitation could be blown away by a gust of wind and forgotten. He imagined waving his hand in casual gesture mimicking the wind blowing the invitation off the coffee table. It would be a nice detail and worthy of the moment.

He would then rise from his seat, collect his papers, explain that he needed to check on the plenary session and wander off leaving her somewhat wide-eyed and wonder-struck perched on the edge of the chaise longe. 'Leave 'em wanting more,' he had learnt from his days in amateur dramatics.

No doubt they would meet at intervals during the rest of the day. He would be relieved the matter had been broached.

She would be somewhat subdued but would valiantly continue to look after the needs of the conference delegates through tea and dinner. He would be thoughtful and chilled. She would start to look at him in a different way. Maybe, he thought, as the day's events came to a close and the delegates and staff retired to their beds, there may be a knock on his bedroom door. She would be standing there, still in shock, his words having eaten into her during the day. He was not expecting, nor wanted, a night time visit with all the trimmings. No, it wasn't appropriate, wasn't right. He didn't want to unveil his inner filth just yet. Besides, if there were prospects, then he wanted to take it slowly. Sometimes things are rushed and become sticky too quickly. He wanted this to last and there would have to be an adjustment in their relationship – from indifferent work colleagues to work colleagues with a difference.

They would spend a few hours talking into the night. She would express her surprise. She would explain the nature of the relationship with her 'boyfriend'. He would explain that he was not pushing, pressing for anything. He was merely drawing the matter to her attention, much as he might draw an error she had made in the office to her attention – with kindness, compassion and patience. He would remind her that he was placing the invitation on a tray as an offering to be considered and reflected upon. Their talk would address some of the shock she was experiencing and she would retire to her room. He would live with a mildly confident hope that perhaps the following few weeks would bear a certain bud of promise. It would flower later perhaps and throw a bit of light relief into his life.

Though the plan had been hatched, like a new born chick, it was largely irrelevant until it had flowered to a point where it would bear fruit. Her departure to pastures new was far from being an impediment to their love story, it was in fact proving to be a catalyst. At last everything was all falling into place. He now had 'A Plan'.

II. A Plan. Plan B.

The weekend of the off-site conference arrived. The delegates themselves arrived at the grand venue on Friday afternoon and were shown to their rooms. He was allocated his own accommodation 300 yards from the main house that served as the conference venue. Lo and behold, she was also allocated a room in same over-spill 'lower-house'. This was, he thought, an excellent turn of events. It was quiet, secure and isolated. The evening conversation on the Saturday night was on schedule. As he unpacked he marvelled at the two comfy armchairs sitting in his room placed in expectation of the life-changing conversation that would occur the evening of the following day, Saturday. He had already casually mentioned to her that he hoped to use the quiet moments during the conference to run through a few things before her departure.

'Oh do we have to?' she had protested. 'Can't it wait 'til next week?'

'Um, no,' he replied, smiling to himself. She had no idea how her life was going to change, he thought.

The conference started well and the first formal dinner arrived on the Friday evening. He was somewhat taken aback to see that she had changed into a figure-hugging, black dress for the occasion. In the office she had usually chosen to worn smart but casual, modest, loose-fitting attire – a character trait that appealed to him. She had a fine figure, but apparently never felt the need to show it off in the workplace. She sought nothing and gained much, including his admiration. As she approached him at the pre-drinks reception he wondered whether it was her presence or the fire crackling in the splendid old fireplace that gave the room a warmth and glow. Nothing need be said, but, yes, she was a mighty fine piece of engineering he noted to himself. If this was what life was like as the lead in a bad romantic novel, he wasn't complaining. It felt good.

Despite being placed at the table to entertain the guests, with more good fortune he found himself seated near her at dinner. He did not actively solicit her attention during the evening but he did make a point of discreetly acknowledging her presence by referring to both his recently purchased Audi two-seater sports car and her Peugeot run-around in a conversation about global warming. He made further sure that she saw a quizzical, cheeky side to his nature as he gently challenged the delegates' learned assumptions while hinting at his own modestly-concealed knowledge of the issues in hand. She laughed. He smiled. Life was good. Such was the drama amidst the politeness of the evening.

After the dinner, as delegates mingled and conversed in the hall by a crackling fire, she sidled up to him.

'I enjoyed your teasing of the delegate about global warming.'

He took the opportunity to joke and share more thoughts on the subject of the warming planet. Thank God for global warming, he mused as they huddled in a corner, marvelling at how comfortable their conspiracy of mirth made him feel. Here he was chatting to a beautiful, charming woman who was, it appeared, perfectly comfortable in his company and intrigued with the workings of his mind. My day has come, he congratulated himself, it's going to be a cake-walk. It had taken a few decades, but...my boat has come in.

They mingled with the delegates over drinks, politely chatting for the next 20 minutes. On two occasions he noted that she had weaved her way towards him to talk more. Then he started to think. And thought turned to panic. Perhaps tomorrow was not the day – the day to broach the matter. Perhaps that very night was the time. Perhaps he didn't need 'A plan', he needed 'Plan B'. Holy crap.

As his mind worked, so life seemed to demand a Plan B.

She offered him a lift in her car through the darkness to the lower-house accommodation. They would be left alone for a few minutes during which time the matter could be broached and the levees breached by the waters of revelation. Life as they had known it would be over.

He had to think quickly. Was this indeed the time? The crowd of delegates thinned and the evening began to wind down. At the allotted moment both he and she moved away from the reception hall and headed to the stairs leading to the basement, his mind turning over the options in his head. Where does he start his monologue – as they walk past the basement kitchens? Or at the point where day turned to night (the basement exit into the courtyard car park)? In the car itself? At the start of the journey? At the end of the journey? Decisions.

As he descended the stairs to the basement he could see the door to the courtyard and the darkness thirty paces away. He thought that by the time he had reached the door he should have started to speak on the matter, banishing her innocence for an eternity. Being casual in such circumstances needed planning, he fretted.

As he worked through the idea of the first few sentences, he couldn't quite believe he was committing himself to such a course of action without proper planning. It was a small step for a man, but a sudden, giant leap for his kind.

The acidic nausea started to seep into his stomach and swirled and splashed around his insides like a wounded alien, almost as if his body did not want to be party to this particular course of action. He noted that he had been here before – in his teens, his twenties and depressingly (but less frequently) in his thirties. Now he had most of his forties laid out before him. He had to slay the alien before it burnt him to death from the inside. He had to follow through. He had to succeed. His boat had docked. Otherwise, how depressing would it be – walking a twenty-five year old home as a man in his mid-forties or early fifties? He knew he had to plough straight on through the pain barrier. Plan A was history. It was a case of now or never. That said, 'never' was an increasingly appealing option, but he knew he had to man up in the next twelve yards. Make that eleven. Besides it was a numbers game – broaching love-stuff. Throw enough rubbish at the wall, some of it has to stick. Surely. He wasn't getting any younger. Although the women were (relative to his age) which arguably was a cause of some embarrassment, but not, he was proud to say, shame.

He knew how he would broach the matter. It would be the 'open invitation' line lifted straight out of Plan A. So, as they reached the door to the darkness of the outside world, he began.

'So, I was going to say, after you leave, I was going to extend an open invitation, if you ever wanted a coffee, bite to eat, then let me know.'

He kept his vocal pace as slow and measured as his stride across the courtyard which was a struggle when his heart was beating out an SOS in Morse code. He kept the direction of his gaze as neutral as possible so the invitation was almost to the cool night as it was to the woman walking beside him to the car.

'Oh, thank you,' she said opening the door of her car. It was the tone (or was it pitch?) in her voice that struck him most. A pitch (or tone) adopted when age was a factor. A pitch often found in old people's nursing-homes. Friendly nurses thanking elderly patients (male or female) for compliments paid to them:

*'You are my favourite nurse. I don't like the
others.'*
'Oh, thank you.'

*'If I was fifty years younger, I'd marry you.
You're beautiful.'*
'Oh, thank you.'

*'I knew something was wrong and then my
bowels opened. I'm glad you are on duty. I
wouldn't want any of the others dealing with my
rubbish.'*
'Oh, thank you.'

With such thoughts popping in his head, he felt he hadn't quite communicated his meaning successfully. By now both he and she were seated in the Peugeot. She was distracted, fiddling with the car ignition. Good thing too, he thought, to have her control complex machinery while he spoke. It helped keep the vibe casual for she wouldn't totally focus on the words lurching out of his mouth because she had to concentrate on keeping the vehicle on the road and away from pedestrians and trees.

He persisted.

'I wanted to say something before you left. I am aware that your circumstances might not permit, but should they change, then, you know, I wanted to know that it would be good.'

Not poetry he knew, but the meaning was there. Somewhere.

The engine sparked into life before settling into a quiet murmur almost as if it too was trying to listen in on what was unfolding.

'Thanks,' she said breezily.

The nursing-home tone seemed to have been diluted somewhat, so there was some progress.

He persisted, again.

She was still living in her pre-9/11 world. Next move was to pay her a compliment without making a move too overt (i.e. slamming the plane into the building). Keep it cool and unthreatening, he thought fighting through the haze. He knew he had to communicate an appreciation for her person. He couldn't just say, 'let's keep in touch'.

Yet, it required thought. In the nanosecond of self-conference, he weighed the options. He couldn't say to her face that he was attracted to her or that she was attractive or that she was gorgeous in a personable sort of way. They had known each other too long. Besides, he was still her line-manager of sorts.

The car turned out of the courtyard into the darkness beyond the security lights for the short drive down to the accommodation, a minute's drive away.

All he had to do was broach the matter. To communicate to her that she was lifted in his consciousness. Put on her radar that she was on his. Plant a seed on her radar. In her plot. Whatever.

'I think you are ...,' he nodded, talking slowly, thinking fast. It mustn't be a throwaway comment. 'I think you are ... nice. And a good ...' he searched for a word that was neither too ordinary nor too risky. Woman? (A dependable word and accurate, but with no 'edge'.) No.

'Egg.'

Surely he'd hit the mark with that one, he thought before suddenly being hit himself with doubt.

The trouble with playing it safe was that it could come across as not a play at all. His mind started to swirl.

She was silent. He had her attention at least and it wasn't an awkward silence, he thought. The evening's mirth was still in their blood (but rapidly being filtered out by his reference to the 'egg' he suspected). Perhaps she had never been called an egg before.

'I just want to put it on your sonar and put it out there.'

His mind was in full swirl now. The reference to an airman's radar tool was the normal choice of metaphor, but was it interchangeable with a submariner's world?

'You're not asking me out on a date are you?' she half-jokingly asked.

He paused with the explicit intention to 'not answer in the negative'. This clever spontaneous trick allowed her to conclude that the answer was indeed leaning toward the affirmative.

'It's just an open invitation. I realise it may be a surprise.' Pause. 'I've a had a few tough years and...'

'Yeah, I know ...'

'I just wanted to express my...admiration..' (much like we have for our armed forces, he thought, though feeling he wasn't again quite hitting the mark with all the military references) '...for you...I think you're nice' (good word, safe) '...and the invitation is there.'

By now they had reached the accommodation and he pointed out the cattle grid and the place to park. She parked the vehicle and they sat for a moment.

'Oh, I'm really flattered,' she said, much quieter now, 'but I don't see you like that.' Her warm tone, now fortunately far from of the nursing-home tone, more like the tone used with a relative of the deceased.

'OK, I know,' he said nodding in a chilled fashion, but it was news to him. 'But the invitation is there.'

He wasn't expecting anything. He just thought he needed to sow his seed in her plot. Sometimes such revelations could shake and reshuffle the order of things he knew, but needed a little time and space to settle afterwards.

He smiled. She smiled a sort of startled smile. The silence was filled by his bleating heart. The car's engine had passed out.

It's all about the sowing, he kept telling himself as he looked at her. A seed hitting the pavement or missing the soil might get blown or washed into a flower-bed at a later date. Nothing was wasted.

The deed of the seed being done, he opened the car door and climbed out.

'As I said, I know your circumstances may not permit it, but ... you know.' He left a meaningful pause. Full of meaning. There was no way he was going to make a move on her that evening, nor give the impression that it was on the cards, regardless of his original intention not to do so.

'I do ask one thing,' he said as he rounded the front of the car and she locked her driver's side, 'that you don't mention this to the others in the office. This information is gold-dust to some of them and I don't want to......'.

'Oh, you know me, you can totally trust me. I'm the soul of discretion,' she said firmly, making a conscious effort to mask her shell-shock. He nodded. He believed her. He trusted her.

And so the matter was broached, the dam breached. With rising levity, he led her up the path to the house. To be sure that she didn't recall the conversation in the isolation of the car, he added a few comments.

'So, there we go. I just want you know that I wouldn't say this off the cuff. I mean every word.' He was as firm and clear as he would have been winding up a meeting at the office. He felt it hit home, but sensed he ought to mix it up using a different tone, a trick he had learnt from watching Pacino. After all, 'mono-tone' he and Pacino most certainly weren't.

'I like you,' he continued, much like he was informing a salesman he liked the vehicle but he wasn't going to pay the asking price. It was not a proposition, just a simple observation. They entered the premises. They talked a little more in the small hallway illuminated by the ageing sixty-watt bulb under a dusty fabric lampshade that had hung undisturbed for decades. He made a point of being chilled. No fuss, no drama. She matched his every move and was perfectly calm. He looked her in the eye in an intentionally unthreatening manner, as they concluded night-time pleasantries.

'Dream of Eric Morcambe', he called up the stairs waving her away and up to bed. She laughed, perhaps nervously he wondered, and disappeared. He entered his own room as relieved as a constipation-clear clergyman celebrating Sunday high mass. Rejoice. Rejoice. All done. What a difference seven minutes make.

As he readied himself for bed and played with his iPad, he noted the restfulness that had come over him before gently dozing off with one thought – 'we'll see what the morning tide brings in'.

III. Plan C. Plan D.

He rose early the following beautiful, bright, sunny morning and ran around the grounds of the stately home. As he jogged down the manicured avenues untouched that day by any other visitor, he felt fresh and relaxed in a way he had not anticipated. After all, Plan A had been scheduled for later that day, Saturday, day two of the conference, but 'job done', he congratulated himself as he jogged back towards his lodgings.

He had done the business in the darkness of the previous day's closing. The world had changed.

They met at breakfast, sitting, chatting cheerfully with colleagues about the grandeur of the house and its furnishings. All he could think about was the conversation the previous night. Or rather all he could *feel* at the breakfast table was the conversation the previous night. Some memories are strong enough to be lived not just recollected. He wondered whether she too was preoccupied by thoughts and re-living the conversation of the previous night. At first he detected a slight reserve, but he wasn't going to dwell on it. Perhaps later in the day there would be a moment to sit and talk a bit more. In the meantime, they enjoyed breakfast and he made a point of being casual while cleverly maintaining a veneer of ease that he had employed for years.

The conference resumed and the plenary sessions began. He kept himself busy working on papers, reports and ushering delegates around the venue. She was also tied up assisting the delegates with queries, dealing with papers and transport enquiries and ushering delegates around the venue. It was after the mid-morning coffee-break before they found themselves chatting with a couple of colleagues in the hall. She was sitting down looking slightly frazzled. A headache, she explained responding to an enquiry from a female colleague. She had not slept she confessed. Oi, oi, he thought to himself, while looking on coolly showing casual concern. Thoughts of Eric Morecambe kept her awake? His confession had probably fried her brain. All that confusion and upheaval. Result.

He was her line manager and there were more brownie points to score. He suggested she go home and spend the night away from the conference before returning on Sunday morning. They could cope without her for the remainder of the day, he explained. She would therefore be fresh for the final day. He suspected that she needed time to think her life through, her world had been turned upside down. Furthermore, he felt that such an offer amply demonstrated his coolness about the situation (a reassuring and attractive quality) coupled with a thoughtfulness about her well-being.

She left at lunchtime on the Saturday with plans to return on the Sunday for a half-day. It would mean there would be no late-night conversation, but it would ensure less stress for everybody.

Sunday arrived, a beautiful sunny day. She was not at breakfast. He was a little concerned that there was no real plan for that day and he would be acting on the hoof again. Though hoof acting had served him well up to that point, he perceived there was risk. He calmed his fears with the knowledge that the years of experience he carried in his breast would serve him well in the hours to come. Nevertheless he knew he thought he might have to lift elements of Plan A for use in 'Plan C: the Return'. He would formulate the plan on sight, assessing her reaction at the moment of arrival to determine whether the matter should be addressed during the conference weekend or revisited back in the office. On reflection he thought that it should be addressed before the delegates left. He couldn't leave it up in the air only for it to come crashing down on him in the office on Monday. No, Sunday was the day. Sending the other work colleague into the plenary sessions would allow him to return to a revised Plan A, perhaps. He could sit and talk things through with her. Although a plan of sorts, she was still nowhere to be seen and the day's sessions were about to start. Perhaps she would arrive mid-morning?

Ten minutes after the beginning of the 9.00 a.m. plenary session he found his male work colleague casually wandering the corridors. Confused, he asked why the younger man wasn't staffing the plenary session only to be informed that she had in fact returned and had volunteered to staff the session herself.

She was avoiding him. Nobody in their right mind would want to sit in a plenary session listening to people talking about things that would never come to pass. Thus, somewhat dejected, he concluded there was little chance of sharing further thoughts with her that morning. He resigned himself to spending the morning walking through the grand rooms alone for he was certainly not inclined to sit and seek support from his junior male colleague. What did the young man know anyway – he had married.

With time on his hands and the sun in full brilliance outside, he exited the building and walked out beyond the immediate perimeter of the house. He leaned on a wooden fence and raised his face to the sky bathing his face in the warmth of the mid-morning sun. Ahead of him lay the rolling green grounds of the house as far as the eye could see. Perhaps the whole episode was another little disappointment to chalk up to experience, he thought. The sun's rays bathed and soothed him, dispersing the anxiety that had been poisoning his once tranquil mind.

Soon, it was morning break-time for the delegates. Perhaps she would go looking for him? Not finding him in the house, she would ask colleagues and they would direct her out to the lawn in front of the house. Behind him he would hear her plimsolls on the gravel before the crunching sound dissolved into the soft tread of woman on grass. He would turn to see her slowly walking up to him and without a word she would join him in silence leaning on the wooden fence warming her fine features in the sun. Or was it the other way round – her features warming the sun? [Sigh.] Inspired by the silence that would linger between them, a half-decent writer could write an epic poem.

'So? How are you?' he would ask with effortless cool.

She would frown and nod, sigh and smile. They would talk. Slowly at first. She would express her shock and confusion. Explain her bewilderment. He would smile and thoughtfully acknowledge her difficulty. The dust would settle from the bomb blast two nights before. An understanding would descend between them for the remaining two weeks in the office and after her departure, and as spring rolled into summer, a warm front might move in.

In the real world (and alone at the fence), he gazed down the road leading away from the house and through an avenue of trees down which (thirty minutes away) waited the ignominy of his regular office job. As he mused in the bright warm glare of the sun, he saw a small (was it a Peugeot?) car leave the courtyard at the back of the house, turn onto a road leading up to the avenue at the end of which lay the outside world. That was quick, he thought. No need for a plan then. She probably realised she didn't really want to face him that day. Was it something he said?

He watched the car recede into the distance. The avenue on which it was travelling was as straight and unforgiving as life, he reflected. Whenever he had tried to turn off his own avenue to invoke a 'choice' for a different life he just ended up in a ditch. Does a man then haul his vehicle back on to the tarmac and journey onwards – along an avenue onto which he felt he had never really turned? Only to conduct a similar manoeuvre with similar results further down the road? Life was, he concluded, an avenue of mythical choices bordered by ditches. He had spent too much time in ditches. Perhaps the ditch was his avenue? Such were his thoughts as he watched the Peugeot melt into the heat haze of the horizon.

Even if he didn't now need a plan for her, he needed a plan of how to haul himself out of this particular ditch: Plan D (which sounded like a plan of his making). He would inevitably meet her at the office the next day and he would have to manage 'the moment' which, like an arthritic man on a mediaeval rack, might be drawn out and painful for the two weeks up to her departure.

Raising his face to the brightest part of the sky he hoped the sun would pierce his flesh, push through his skull and slowly burn away the plans and hopes he had made for her, for them. Her image and his plans fried, their particle remains would be consigned to swirl about the galaxies.

Conscious of time, and noting that it was nearly the end of the morning break, he turned and moped off back to the house. He would have to show (and hide) his face for a few minutes.

He walked as slowly as possible to give the sun as much time as possible to warm his back before entering the cool sobriety of the house. Delegates were busy milling about drinking tea and chatting. He nodded and smiled and kept an eye out for any problems. There were none. He would check in with his junior male colleague to ensure the final plenary session before lunch was staffed. Coffee in hand he found his colleague at the entrance of the library preparing the papers for the final plenary session, but almost immediately he was distracted by the sight of a slim figure of young woman further down the library.

It was her.

She was laying out the papers on the table. Something inside him lifted, turned over, only to collapse in on itself again.

His thoughts were broken by the male colleague pointing out the cartoons the delegates had been drawing on their pads, a number of which were rather saucy.

'Oh I know, aren't they awful,' he heard her say, finding her now standing at his elbow.

Stunned, he cranked up his cheer by the power ten, 'Let's have a look.'

The three of them flipped through the cartoon doodles like three youngsters discovering porn in the playground. Oh, to be young and flippant again, he thought as the morning break concluded and the delegates started to file back into the room. The three staffers went their separate ways and a relief washed over him. Perhaps his future was not off-road just yet.

Refreshed and seeking refreshment, he picked up a coffee in the nearby hall and watched the last of the delegates return to the library for the final session. It was not long before he found himself with her in a lounge, just as he had originally planned. Having enquired about the welfare of the delegates and how the first plenary session of the day had gone, he drifted around the room looking at the view of the warm day outside.

'Thanks for the chat the other night,' he said feeling as cool as a cat on a hot tin roof. 'Did it freak you out?'

'Just a bit.'

He smiled, warmly and carefully.

'Well, it's an open invitation, if you ever want to,' he said nodding.

This was looking like Plan A, so he employed the hand gesture of offering the invitation on a tray, 'but if you want,' he continued, 'you can let it blow away in the wind,' using the gesture lifted directly out of the original plan. Nice.

'No pressure,' he said forcing himself not to look at her expectantly. She nodded and smiled, possibly feeling six earth pressures to her every square inch. Ah, the stress of casual interaction.

He apologised for his use of the phrase 'good egg' two nights before confessing he didn't quite know from where it had come. He was fully aware it wasn't a winner and by inadvertently using it he didn't want to give the impression that he was in fact a loser. She graciously accepted his apology, dispelling nothing.

'I just think you're …,' (he thought carefully, adamant he was not going to liken her to farm produce or reference military technology of any sort), 'supercool,' he said firmly, and, he hoped, winningly. Even if it was a little '1970s', it could qualify as 'retro' (and therefore valid) to her generation. He talked a little more, moving the conversation away from that about which they were both inwardly convulsing.

The conference wound down in the hours that followed and nothing more was said. All remaining interaction was uneventful and reasonable.

IV. Plan E.

As he watched her drive away from the venue at the end of the conference he calculated that there were twelve days left before their working lives parted forever, at least four of which did not apply because of his annual leave and the intervening weekend. That left eight. Of the eight, there was one day in London supporting a busy work-related function leaving seven of relatively normal interaction. He suspected she would take her remaining holiday leave which would reduce the number yet further. How many days were left, he wasn't sure. He knew he must not rush it. He must demonstrate that their relationship could be normal and chilled. The next three working days in the office should be left untouched, unsullied by words, he concluded. He estimated there was a window of four days in which to raise and explore matters further. A sober play for affection. He could use the small matter of the London-function forty-eight hours later to advance his (and, dare he say, her) interests. It needed a plan.

Plan E: London. After an evening function in London, the day would end with a bus journey back to their home town dropping off work colleagues along the way. Raising the matter during the day was not an option. Indifferent interaction during the event was required. However, in the quietness of the return coach journey there might be an opportunity for quiet conversation. Seventeen people returning on a forty-four-seater coach would allow co-workers to move about the vehicle. It had happened before. When travelling to school matches in his teens, friends would swap seats and talk. It could just work. Having had a few days to mull over the news, she would want to talk things through? Surely? Even if it were to express her surprise and share her bewilderment.

The plan was taking shape. Halfway through the journey, with the inner lights dimmed, the coach would be lost in the midnight darkness of the motorway. The steady rock and sway of the coach would have lulled most of the travellers into a light slumber. He would be leaning against the window watching the road lines streak past and the blackness of the sky undulating against the yet blacker tree-line. Headphones on, he would listen to the stuttering reception of Melody FM's Love Hour as the coach departed the capital. Suddenly he would be stirred from his stupor by the weight of the seat next to him suddenly taking the weight of a body. Lifting his heavy head from the vibrating window, he would turn to see that she had left the company of a sleeping colleague to join him.

He would note her arrival with a pursed smile of acknowledgement.

Come to haul me out of the ditch? he wouldn't say.

He wouldn't remove his headphones and, in comfortable silence, they would sit. Old friends together. After a while, he would pull out his smartphone and using a notes-function, tap out a few words before handing the device to her.

Still in shock?

She would take the phone from him, read, and type a short reply. He would note the smooth long, womanly fingers, perfectly manicured, moving quickly and skilfully over the keypad. She hands the phone back to him:

A bit.

He takes the device from her and types.

Glad you know.

He shows her the screen, before typing again.

U OK?

He hands her the phone (pleased to have demonstrated his knowledge of modern SMS-speak) and watches in suppressed wonder as the screen illuminates the features that weakened him almost to a point of sadness.

Once upon a time it was moonlight, then the light from flickering fires that imbued the features of a love interest with mystery and wonder. Now it was the faint hue from electronic devices. From silver, to flickering golden yellows and reds, to sickly green. Could chaste moments of romance really truly exist now that moonlight and firelight had been banished? Humanity had lost something in the light. Liquid crystal was not as poetic as it sounded.

He reads her reply.

Confused.

He replies.

[Smiley face] Understood.

They exchange more messages each avoiding answers but ever so gradually moving the elephant towards the door. She returns to her original seat after half and hour. He would text her a 'goodnight' as they approach home. She responds in kind and before the midnight hour the seed sown four days earlier has borne the smallest, but greenest, of shoots.

That was the plan.

As the bus wound its way through night-time London, he sat alone but for a cardboard box of unused flyers for company next to him. As Melody FM played love ballads late into the night, he stared at the blank screen of his new smartphone.

Bugger, isn't there anyone I can text? he muttered to himself.

She sat beside her female secretarial colleague several rows behind him, so the plan wasn't redundant yet, but at no point during the journey did he feel the rustle of the cardboard box being moved from the seat beside him. Nor did he hear the sigh of the seat as it welcomed the weight of a soft, warm body. No, the journey was unremarkable. No metaphor or simile required.

He found himself wondering about other people's lives. Where and how had they found turns off their own ditch-bordered avenues? The world allowed some men to dream then fly to the moon. For the rest, pacing the planet in straight lines was the rule, but straight lines on a globe were circles, he noted. The more we learn about nature's laws, the more they seem to mock us, he thought: walk in a straight line only to end up going in circles. Someone somewhere was laughing himself silly, he spat inside his head. The world of choice was nonsense. It didn't exist. Dreams, thoughts, plans, whatever. The question was: how does one rid oneself of the imagined world that rotted the brain, dissolved time and amount to nothing?

The night was not over for they were scheduled to disembark at the same stop. And so they did. She glided off the coach ahead of him and turned left towards a car park. Standing on the pavement as the coach moved off behind him he watched as the night swallowed her up. He turned and walked the final mile in the other direction towards his own vehicle parked in a residential street a mile away. Maybe, just maybe, she might pass him, stop and offer him a lift to his own car. But, no. Or yes, and no. Her car did indeed pass him. It didn't stop. It too was swallowed up into the night.

V. Plan F.

Plan F. It would have to be the work environment – something he had been trying to avoid for a number of reasons: too many people milling about, the line-manger-thing and finally, the head-space thing. One's head is in the workspace at work, not the love-space. But it had to be done. The very next day he would raise the matter. In the kitchenette in a casual break, mid-morning. Certainly not in the afternoon, that would be a killer of a wait. All their interaction appeared to be in casual situations in his 'other-world'. It always worked there, so keep it casual, he thought. The trouble with the real-world was that he would have to contrive the 'casualness' of the 'break'.

The plan gradually took shape and the timing identified: mid-morning on Thursday, her penultimate day. She would, by chance, find him in the kitchenette casually dunking his tea-bag into his tea in a wholly unthreatening manner. They would exchange carefully-crafted casual hellos and smiles. Just as he was nonchalantly dropping the tea-bag into the waste-bin, he would carefully, casually ask after her (that is her mental state, the implication being the fall-out from the atomic bomb he had dropped on her eleven days earlier).

'OK?'

'OK,' she would nod.

'You're not grumpy with me, are you?' he would ask.

'No,' she shakes her head. 'Why would I be?'

He would try his best pursed-lips-inverted-smile thing and perhaps raise an eyebrow.

'You know I sometimes head down the road at lunchtime on a Thursday and get a pizza deal at Flame and Dough. If you'd like to join me, it would be good to chat and I could explain a bit more.'

'I don't think so,' she would say, her eyes narrowing.

He wouldn't fight. He'd play it cool and let her get used to the idea.

'Well, it would be nice if you did. I'm there by one o'clock usually.'

And with that he would exit the kitchenette unintentionally leaving his cooling chocolate bar in the fridge. He wouldn't go back for it.

At lunchtime he would make his way to the pizza restaurant and wait. The deed had been done. He wasn't going to do nor expect any more. He was spent. Shot. There were only so many bullets in the magazine-clip of his love gun.

As he was calmly and casually looking through the menu a young woman would slip into the chair across the table from him. Slightly short of breath and a tinge of colour in her cheeks, she would remove her coat. He would smile and nod in an unthreatening manner (perhaps with pursed lips) and finger the waitress. (He meant 'beckon', and cursed himself as he desperately tried to shake the shameful image from his carefully imagined moment.)

They would chat about her new job, her plans and other stuff (of no consequence at all but romantically very appropriate). Towards the end of the hour he would raise the thorny issue of the big elephant squashed up in the corner of the establishment.

'As you know it has been a difficult few years what with this and that. I'm planning to treat myself to a pick-me-up or two. The Audi sports car was the first pick-me-up. The third will be a sunset. All I need now is the second – a brunette in the passenger seat,' he would say without dipping an eyebrow.

'I've been checking,' he would continue after leaving his previous sentence hanging in the air. 'There are sunsets almost every day. I have the vehicle. All I need is the brunette.'

Granted, it would depend on the delivery, but he thought he could pull if off. Some ladies might dismiss it as a clumsy line, but she knew him better. He would follow it with a low-key, puppy-dog look of innocence (with perhaps a hint of vulnerability for good measure).

She would squint at him – protesting outwardly but melting inwardly.

'I thought you might be grumpy,' he'd say. 'I didn't want to make you grumpy.'

'I wasn't grumpy,' she would reply slowly.

He would give her a look artfully raising a quizzical eyebrow for the first time.

'No I wasn't,' she would protest almost making his point for him. He didn't want to make it difficult for her. They would leave the restaurant, the stage having been set. Act One nicely concluded.

And so, the penultimate day, Thursday, arrived. It was Plan F or nothing. He wasn't sure he could orchestrate a meeting in the kitchenette, so, with an 'oh-holy-cow-to-hell-with-it' spasm of spontaneity, he decided to bring it forward. At approximately 9.30 in the morning, thirty minutes into the working day, he found himself alone in the office with her. The corridor outside seemed quiet too. No, he wasn't going to delay. He spun round on his chair and rose to his feet.

'How are you?'

'Fine.'

'Over the shock?'

He knew he had twenty-nine hours to wrap this up.

'Er yeah, sort of.'

He was now on his feet and heading for the door that led to the corridor which led to the kitchenette where he could dunk his tea. He didn't know why, but talking on the move kept it casual. He paused by the door and spun round carefully positioning himself for the Plan F off-the-cuff observation.

'You know I sometimes head to the Pizza restaurant down the road on Thursdays to make the most of their Thursday pizza offer. You are welcome to join me, if you like, it would be good to talk about …'

'I think everything's been said,' she quipped, cutting him off.

Momentarily off-balance, he regained his composure and his move.

'I'd like to give a bit of background…,' he continued.

'I think everything has been said.' Even firmer this time.

There was a finality about her tone that sort of killed his follow-up sentence and any thought he might give to a closing statement along the lines of….he couldn't remember. It was a blast of air cold enough to give a woolly mammoth the chills. For years friends had encouraged him to evolve, to 'say more, express more,' but when he did find himself in a place to share some thoughts all he got was a face-full of arctic wind. He was prepared to evolve, but it appeared evolution had itself moved on. Maybe he heard his friends wrong? Maybe it was in fact 'oblivion' and not 'evolution' that he needed to embrace.

It was a shame. He had wanted to communicate at least one thing. Regardless of her grumpiness, he wanted to say (and for her to note) that she was appreciated. Supercool. She may not want to hear it, but he wanted it noted by the cosmos at least, even if it were a giggling witness. His appreciation for another human form should not pass unremembered, but in that real-world moment, he felt that a mature response was required. He shouldn't press it.

'OK,' he breathed and nodded and peeled himself away from the doorframe on which he had been ever so casually leaning, and headed to the kitchenette.

That was easy, he thought. Clarity is good.

Standing in the kitchenette, slowly stirring his coffee and squashing the floating coffee granules against the mug's rim, he let the kitchenette plan dissolve into the cosmic ether. Plans really have no currency at all he thought as he stirred. He recalled the observation that the happiest people were those who didn't make plans which made sense to him because he felt pretty miserable.

Sigh. Crap.

'Sigh', 'Crap' – two words which in his youth had been distant relatives were now old drinking buddies slumped at the bar of middle age. Yes, at least there's clarity, he thought.

There was nothing more to do in the remaining thirty-two hours other than endure the inevitable gathering at which a leaver's card would be presented to her. He had made a point of being the last to sign the office card. He included the word 'Supercool' in his message to remind her of the conference cleverly followed by '[sigh]'. The card was presented at a gathering of twenty people at which he fidgeted, chatted amiably with colleagues all the while noting his nausea bubbling away. Although he made a point of not avoiding looking in her direction, he did wonder if, when she opened the card, smiled and laughed politely at the messages, her eye might search for his comment on the card and then him in the room. The Friday afternoon ticked away and he made a plan to leave the office early allowing him to be in control of the goodbyes. Better to fake than be faked on.

VI. Plan G.

It was the final plan. A week earlier he had purchased a small box of chocolate biscuits of a brand he knew she liked. He had thought that such a gift would demonstrate that he was a good listener (her having confided her weakness for the biscuit brand months before). His bag packed, his jacket donned, he intended to hand over the wrapped box of biscuits as his parting act. As the moment of departure approached he left untouched in his desk drawer the card he had also purchased for the final goodbye, thinking it might be too much. After all, the old adage, 'always leave them wanting more' might still yet apply. He had been looking for a card with a simple artful drawing of a couple of steaming coffee cups. 'Nuff said – the invitation was still open. Disappointingly, he was unable find such a card. All he could find was a Banksy graffiti image of a hooligan throwing a bunch of flowers. Nice. Appropriate. However, the image (and thought) of a middle-aged man flogging a dead horse being more appropriate had popped into his head. In fact, why not a man flogging a dead horse with a bunch of flowers? Nice. Feeling that it was best not to give her the opportunity for such a thought to enter her own mind, he let the Banksy card lie in the drawer undisturbed in its plastic envelope. Nevertheless, it was humiliating. Humiliation by the other-world – a world that existed only inside his head. Humiliation by unicorn. Nice.

Ironically he had been her referee for her new post and his reference had been glowing. As he left the office on that final day he handed her a copy for her own future use. Perhaps she would think again when she read it.

Plan G: he would walk to the lift alone, seeing him leave she would soften (the biscuits, the referee's letter) and run after him. She would express her gratitude for helping her career development and providing the reference to melt all references. He would mention the invitation again and apologise for making her grumpy. She would protest that she wasn't grumpy. There would be a little chat then a little hug. They would part. She would be confused, but the sown seed was on the radar, their future together well and truly soiled. It would just be a matter of time.

There were flashes of alternative partings: one being when she was ceremoniously escorted to the lift by her colleagues leaving him gulping like a goldfish behind the chattering crowds. No, he was having none of it. He knew he had to get creative, and get out quick, before the hullabaloo.

He packed his bag early and made to leave before five o'clock. Making sure other colleagues were present, he loudly announced his early departure and humble sadness that she was leaving and handed over the wrapped box of biscuits, wishing her all the best. With jacket buttoned up, bag slung over his shoulder, he even leaned down to the seated young woman and gave her a one-armed hug. She knew exactly what he was attempting and complied. A one-arm hug, from the side, while seated. An observer would think nothing of it. Two colleagues bidding each other goodbye. Sadly that was just what it was. They were colleagues who would probably never see each other again. His remaining two score years and her three score years on the planet although temporally simultaneous would be spatially distinct from one another (perhaps by no more than half-a-dozen miles). Such was life on Evil Planet Earth. All that energy and planning. Maybe at the end of a long life he might recall her when flicking through the diaries of his middle-aged prime as his needs were tended to by the nursing-home's really rather charming nurse.

As he passed the following days pottering around his house he contemplated the likelihood of receiving, six months later, a SMS text on his phone asking how he was. It would be the start of an exchange of messages that might indeed lead to coffee. At which point he would congratulate himself for playing aloof. He had played his hand just right after all. The Maestro.

Yet, in a moment of clarity or despair (what's the difference? discuss) he deleted her number from his phone. She was gone. That was it.

He might, of course, receive a SMS text later in the year from an 'unknown number'. So, he concluded, it was no bad thing he had written down her contact details before deletion. After all, it gave him options that might require him to come up with a plan.

Fear of Lions

– I – **Week One, Monday**

'*That* is why,' he said. '*That* is why.'

'I must ... front my ....,' she struggled.

' 'Confront' ... it means: stand up to. Meet head on. Fight.'

'Confront...my fears. Don't be afraid of anything?' she whispered, her eyes fixed on her wise counsel.

He shook his head solemnly. 'No, nothing.'

'Really?' she gasped, her face grave, full of seriousness. More seriousness than he could ever muster.

'Really,' he said reassuringly. He would never tire of the role of the doting uncle. It was wondrous to watch a very young person struggling to comprehend the world just three years after having emerged screaming and blinking into the light. She seemed to listen to him. Not many others did. Her mother didn't. Not really. There would be no seriousness in his sister's face when he spoke. No, she (and others) would smile and nod when he would say something, but they wouldn't really be listening to him. Not like Maia. Whether it was a personality thing or an age thing, he did not know. Maybe she would roll her eyes too in years to come when he tried to impart pearls of wisdom, but that was a few years away (at least two, possibly three, judging on the development of her older brother and sisters).

'What are you afraid of?' he whispered leaning in.

She thought. Her big brown eyes locked on his, but her thoughts were distant.

Silence.

Eventually her gaze fell away from him as her thoughts deepened. He wondered what images, experiences she was turning over in her little mind. He wasn't going to rush her. It was nice to see a little person locked in deep, deep thought.

'Lions,' she said.

'Lions?' he replied, suppressing his amusement with a feigned startledness. He had been expecting 'the dark', or 'big rabbits' or maybe even daddylonglegs, but no, it was lions.

'It's true. They are scary.'

'Very scary,' she nodded gravely.

He wondered whether she had ever seen a lion in the flesh or was it all from watching nature documentaries on television. He wasn't going to pry. He was just enjoying the seriousness of the little lady in front of him.

'You're very clever,' she said.

'Oh, modesty forbids...' he said with a wave of his hand.

The little, grave face turned into a little confused one.

'Thank you,' he continued not wanting to explain away the moment.

'You should be a king one day.'

'Oh, I don't think so. Nobody listens to me.'

'I do,' Maia protested.

'I know, but nobody is going to call me 'Your Majesty' or 'Mr President' any day soon. And I have I to learn to live with that.'

'What is a President?'

'A very clever man (or woman) who is very wise and who becomes a leader.'

And that was the Monday of the first week (of the four) that changed his life forever.

– II – Week One, Thursday

Three days later on the Thursday of the first week (of the four that changed his life forever) he was round again at his sister's home. Not living far away and trying to be the helpful sort, he would drop by the house to help out, while making sure he kept himself out of the way when necessary. His sister's home was where he felt comfortable.

'I'm here to assist,' he would say. 'Anything.'

His role (as he understood it) principally included distracting the children and shopping for food. Having arrived at the house with two bags of shopping, he noted that preparations for a family excursion were advanced. He placed the shopping bags on the kitchen table and awaited further instructions. Maia's older brother (Marcus, twelve) and sister (Emily, eight) were making their customary fuss of putting their coats on in the hall. He heard his own sister upstairs trying to coordinate the movements of another sister, Gemma (eleven). Within a minute a frazzled mother descended the stairs and entered the kitchen.

'Can you look after Gemma, she's not coming.'

'Sure.'

He spotted a suited and booted serious-looking Maia waiting patiently and expectantly at the bottom of the stairs. Normally it was Maia who would be the cause of any delay when the family was leaving the house, but not today, apparently.

'Where are you going?' the uncle asked Maia who looked as solemn as a three year old girl could.

She dipped her head in a grave fashion and in a firm, hushed voice, replied, 'to the zoo'.

'To the zoo? Ooo, that's exciting,' he replied encouraged that a young person could be so interested in the outside world when computer screens abounded. Who knows where such a curiosity might lead? Nowadays, he thought, nobody over sixteen would be as committed to the idea of a visit to the zoo as Maia appeared to be.

She looked around her, probably for her mother who was firmly telling Gemma to behave while Marcus and Emily fought over the front door locks. Thus it was that Maia and her uncle were left alone in their own private moment.

The young girl stepped forward and whispered with the greatest of solemnity: 'to confront my fears'.

'Oh, OK' he said nodding, knowing that somewhere in the back of his mind that this made sense. If he wasn't mistaken he had been sharing pearls of wisdom with his niece earlier that week. (Just before he captained England to victory (seven goals to four) over Spain captained by her (latterly tear-soaked) brother Marcus).

'Now you behave and listen to your uncle,' the children's mother said to Gemma.

'Why?' the girl whined, stamping her foot.

'Yeah, why?' the uncle asked himself. He noted that his sister didn't respond and wondered whether she was lost for a good argument.

Preparations completed, the young busy woman escorted three of her children out of the house. So it was that that Thursday (of the first week of the four that changed his life forever) started quietly but became the busiest (and probably most momentous) of those twenty-eight days.

It was when the front door opened that it all hit him. It was like a bomb going off, but with the sound and visuals not quite synced. Perhaps he had heard the cars draw up outside the house and the muffled crying through the doubled-glazed windows, he didn't know. It hadn't registered. But now it did, everything did. A screaming, wailing Emily, a sobbing Marcus, their whimpering mother and gruff voices trying to speak gently. He was on his feet trying to adjust to the sound and fury when the policemen and policewomen suddenly filled the hall. Some officers were trying to escort the children who, if they weren't crying, were screaming and bellowing. Everybody around him seemed to know what was happening therefore for a few seconds it seemed odd (even stupid) to ask what was going on. Just when he thought he had a legitimate right to ask, one police officer approached him.

'Are you Mr Winterbourne?'

'No, no, I'm the brother. My sister's divorced. Her ex has moved to Canada. He's out of the picture. What's going on?'

Suddenly there was another scream to his left. They looked. He saw Marcus standing in front of his sister, Gemma. He wasn't speaking but looked as if he had just spoken. Whatever he had said, it cannot have been good.

Almost in slow motion he watched as Gemma expelled the last of her air before taking in a sharp breath which fuelled another piercing scream which itself morphed into a wail. Within seconds, she was at full throttle.

The policeman took the confused uncle's arm and guided him into the kitchen. A pale policewoman followed, desperately trying to maintain a firm professional gaze but without much luck. Within moments he found himself in the kitchen standing opposite two tense, breathless police officers with a background of wailing from the dining room next door (Gemma), accompanied by heavy sobbing (Marcus) both of which were echoed by further delirious wails and sobs coming from the sitting room (his own sister and other niece, Emily).

'What is this?' he whispered, his mouth dry.

'Your niece,' he policeman responded. 'Maia.'

'Yes?' He nodded. 'She's gone to the zoo.'

176

'Yes,' the policeman sighed in reply. 'There's been an incident at the zoo.'

The uncle didn't say anything. The three of them knew that he had nothing to add to the conversation at this stage, so the policeman continued.

'Maia momentarily separated herself from your sister and climbed a fence and into an animal enclosure.'

'Which enclosure?'

The policewoman took a deep breath, paused at the intake of air then delivered the news on the exhale. 'The lion enclosure.'

The uncle was waiting for the next line. There was nothing, just pale faces.

'Is she OK?'

'She was attacked.'

'And?'

Both officers looked perplexed. Wasn't it clear already?

'There were six of them. She was three years old.'

Pause.

'I'm sorry,' the policeman muttered.

Gemma stormed into the kitchen. 'Is it true? Maia's been eaten by lions?'

The Thursday of the first week (of the four that changed his life forever) did have another eight hours to run, but it was a blur and the most dramatic day of the twenty-eight indeed.

– III – Week One, Saturday

The Saturday of the first week (of the four that changed his life forever) was, in comparison, very, very quiet. There were people in the house, but everybody was quiet. Some people were in a room on their own but they were very quiet. In other rooms there were four, five, even six people in the room and they were very quiet. Even the feet padding from room to room were trying to be quiet. Perhaps all the shouting was going on in their heads.

As an uncle, he was 'in attendance', but he would rather have been elsewhere. He had compromised. He sat on the damp garden bench staring out across the fields at the lifeless green landscape and colourless overcast sky. There wasn't even shading in the cloud, it was all a monotone off-white colour. In fact it wasn't really cloud and there wasn't really colour. It was just stuff. A sort of blanket of gauze. Nothingness.

He had been thinking of only one thing in the previous 48 hours: him sitting on a sofa on the previous Monday looking into the eyes of a serious three year old digesting one of his very own pearls of wisdom.

The door clicked behind him and he heard a few soft rubber-soled steps on the patio slabs approach him, some of which were interspersed with little splashes as the cheap shoes stepped into water gathered on the uneven surface of the slabs.

A woman sat down next to him. He didn't look at her. The grass in front of him was much more interesting. So many blades (and each at a slightly different angle). If scientists measured them they would probably find that they were all completely unique. It was an interesting hypothesis. Perhaps he should conduct a study. After all he wasn't going anywhere. Possibly ever.

He knew who the woman was – one of the victim support volunteers sent to torture victims' families. Normally he would have the strength to keep such annoyances from the door, but he was too weak. That's how they get in, he thought. He then felt a hand on his knee and suddenly found himself praying for strength (and then, to his shame, for a lion).

One reason he wanted to be out of the house was that there was discussion about funeral arrangements. A funeral without a body? Coffins for three year olds were small anyway, but, according to what was not being said, there was nothing left of Maia. There was talk of killing the six animals and filling a coffin with half-digested pieces which was followed by objections on the grounds that the lions were endangered animals following their natural instincts.

'If you want to talk about anything, we are here,' the nuisance muttered.

'I know' he said, disgusted at himself for not summoning enough contempt and now conscious of the water seeping into his underwear as the wooden bench claimed his afternoon.

– IV – Week Two, Monday

Monday of the second week (of the four that changed his life forever) felt like how things were going to be for a while – people in the house – who all behaved as though they belonged there. Existing in a constant state of stunned composure (that he did not consider healthy) he thought the visitors' presence was survivable in the short term. They included: police liaison, press liaison, charity supporters, grief counsellors, neighbours known to him and neighbours unknown to anybody. The professionals arguably had a justifiable presence; the others less so, he suspected their 'recruitment' practices (as such) were less discerning. They were more meddlers than supporters. Now, rather than being a positive force in the house, he felt like an observer. His irritation was compounded by a suppressed sense that he had no right to be irritated. Whenever he moved from one room to another he would feel a hand on his arm or his chest followed by a slow expiration of breath towards him before the hand was removed. Consoling it wasn't.

He was really there for his sister and to keep an eye on the children. He moved about the house in a stupor. He had been offered sedatives, but declined. If his sister was sedated someone needed to be clear-headed for the kids (if clear-headed was the word). There were a few interruptions to the stupor, however, including the news that the zoo's lion handler had been arrested which was followed by news that, as an alternative to death, the lions might be moved to a zoo in Asia.

'Taking Maia in their tummies with them?' Emily had screamed in protest.

He didn't have the heart to say that it was probable that Maia had worked her way through their system by then.

There was talk of a statement being issued to the press by a family member and, before he knew it, he was standing in front of a counsellor, police liaison and press liaison officers, being advised that his sister, Maia's mother, could not do it. She was too distraught. No shit Sherlock, were the words he ached to utter, but the lone thread of maturity and reasonableness kept him quiet. All his audience could see was a studious, beaten, sad uncle trying to cope with his despair.

'Your sister wants you to do it,' the press liaison person said. 'Would you?'

He hankered after a different time when the world was a place where a man could have stepped forward and, with a right hook, knocked the press person out cold, with the police officer doing nothing, other than nodding in sympathy. No, times had changed.

'Me? No,' he said.

'Do it for your sister. For Maia. She wouldn't want the lions killed.'

This confused him, because the thirty-year old press liaison person never knew Maia. For all he knew Maia would want the animals dead, even eaten themselves.

'You didn't know Maia' he whispered.

'But we can know her memory,' the woman replied.

What the holy hell that meant, he didn't know. Again he hankered after a long forgotten time of hooks and upper-cuts. He shook his head and that was enough. The press liaison woman moved away followed by the police officer and grief counsellor, but not before each stroked his arm.

He felt bad for doubting their motives. Perhaps they are not all nuisances, he thought. And with that he returned to moving softly around the people who were loitering in his sister's house until the light faded and died (no doubt of exhaustion).

Late, late in the evening he emerged from one armchair in a dark corner of the lounge. His sister was curled up under blankets on the sofa. He had not really spoken to her in the last six days. Even six months. He wanted to talk to her, now, soon. About Maia. But looking at her resting in the pillows and clutching Maia's toy penguin, he thought it could wait. He wished he could be there for his sister as a brother should. He crept over to her and softly planted a kiss on her forehead.

She stirred, her eyes opened.

'Sorry. I thought you were asleep.'

She was peaceful. She did not have to smile. She did not have to nod. The embers of their childhood understanding remained. It was a time, a world, an age ago – before the drama of the teen-age, before the years of college drama, before the disappointment of the early career period, before the hullabaloo of the young family enlightenment and finally before the dark age of bereavement. It was the sudden and violent departure of a small family member that regressed them back to their childhood; a childhood when they were each other's worlds.

'I'm going now. I'll be back in the morning. Sleep.'

His sister stirred again.

'They want someone to give a press conference. Say a few words about Maia.'

He nodded. He was confident she would forget by the morning.

'I know she cared for you,' his sister continued. 'And listened to you. Will you do it?'

He said nothing, just smiled. If she says any more, there was a chance she would remember in the morning.

'She thought you were very clever. It is one of the things she said to me in the car on the way to the zoo.'

And that was the last thing he remembered about the second day of the second week (of the four that changed his life forever).

– V – Week Two, Wednesday

When the third day of the second week (of the four that changed his life forever) actually began was difficult to say. In part because he couldn't remember what happened before 11.00 a.m.. He knew it was eleven o'clock because the press liaison officer kept referring to the time. It felt as though it started when he found himself sitting in front of a bank of a hundred reporters each one clutching an electronic device to record either the grieving uncle's thoughts or, better still, their own. There were five people at the table in front of the crowd, why he was put in the middle he did not know. The police officer had spoken, but the family liaison person had said nothing. The health and safety person (who had never visited the house) said something, but whatever it was, it was unremarkable. And there was someone else who he might have known for a fleeting moment, but then forgot. She might have been the deaf signage person but it was odd because she did nothing with her hands. She just kept nodding.

He might have said a few words himself, but only out of politeness and nothing he hadn't said to other people he had found wandering about his sister's house in recent days. So it was strange that all the questions coming from the crowd seemed to be directed to him.

'You were close. Do you know why she did it?' a voice emerged from the writhing mass in front of him. He looked around, looking for the source of the voice, nobody else did though, they all kept looking at him.

'Do you know why she did it? Climbed into the lion enclosure?'

Why? he thought.

Perhaps his face said it all because another voice from another part of the room asked another question:

'She liked lions?'

'No, no, no, he muttered, his voice falling away. 'She was... scared of them.'

There was a murmur around the dark swirling mass. They seemed confused.

'She was fearless?' asked a reporter from somewhere.

'.. she was ...,' he heard his voice fade.

'Fearless?' the reporter repeated.

'Confronting her fears, I suppose,' he whispered, his eyes falling to the table, his words drifting toward the mass.

Then there was sudden movement beside him and a woman's voice emerged from the person:

'Maia loved and feared lions,' she started...

Which he thought was odd, because the woman to whom the voice belonged, was another person who had never met Maia, the inquisitive and serious young girl into whose eyes he had been staring only ten days before. Tomorrow it would be eleven days in the past. Not long afterwards it would fourteen days, the week after that would be over twenty. The number would always rise now, never fall. It would move relentlessly in one direction. Who knows, eventually the number would reach over a thousand. To think there would be a day when the moment he looked into her eyes would be separated by a thousand of its cousins, each one chipping away at the vividness of the memory until Maia became almost a work of fiction.

'She was confronting those fears, something which we must all do. We could all learn from...,' the woman continued, which again struck him as odd.

He sensed movement to his right. Was it the woman at the end of the table who was nodding. Do all these people appear after the death of a person? A death of a child? Do they not concern themselves with living children?

Speaking of the living. His thoughts turned to his sister. He needed to talk to her. To explain the last conversation he had had with Maia, but he had to choose his moment. Perhaps understanding Maia's thinking on the day would lead to some reconciliation to the loss. The last thing he wanted was for there to be a lingering doubt in his sister's mind that she might somehow be responsible. Nevertheless he was also aware it would not be a pleasing conversation and might well harm his own relationship with Maia's mother. But he owed it to Maia and he owed it to Maia's brother and sisters. They needed a fully functioning mother. Uncles were optional.

'Which makes me think that Maia would want the lions to live. To live with a fear of lions is better than lions living in fear .... of imminent death ..,' the person next to him concluded solemnly.

Again, what was the woman talking about? Who was she?

– VI – Week Two, Friday

The Friday of the second week (of the four that changed his life forever) marked an end and a beginning. It marked the end of Maia's time with the family and the beginning of a time without Maia. The press attention would be ascribed to Maia-time. He would not want it to contaminate the next stage. The noise in the head and house would all quiet down now and the new phase would begin. The 'time beyond Maia', at which point the little girl would be a historical document in the lives of his sister, and Maia's siblings, Emily, Marcus and Gemma. Living with such an unchanging historical artifact in an ever-changing life would be the challenge, especially for the growing children. That was the next phase. Right now 'Maia-time' was coming to an end in the form of edited footage of her funeral. Images of a church, a graveyard, a cortege, crowds dressed in a dark colours, a priest and finally the uncle standing in front of a congregation reading a few words from a piece of crumpled paper. Her favourite, clever uncle.

He watched as the television news report was interspersed with clips of women clutching handkerchieves to their faces as they watched him speak on a large screen erected outside the church (something of which he had not been aware). The televised funeral differed from his own memory of the morning. The camera angle (from the back of the church) captured the image of him standing in front of rows of heads of hair, the odd pale scalp and even a few 'nice' hats worn only on special occasions (visits by television camera crews). It did not show what he had seen – ashen, crying faces many of which he did not recognise. Even the nodding woman could be seen standing, dabbing her eyes at the back of the church and nodding. Most of the people in the church had not known Maia. There were some cousins, but otherwise it was the local community and people from the support services. They would not recognise Maia if she had walked in and sat amongst them. But that was impossible. Some people thought she was in the little white box. She wasn't. There might have been a few pieces, but not many.

He hadn't really wanted to speak at the funeral. He wanted to distance himself from the episode altogether, but when the matter had arisen in another little gathering in his sister's sitting room, he felt the jostling for position by others. In a fit of fervour, he agreed that he would give a small talk but only to prevent those unknown to Maia from making a career-defining, Facebook-relevant, Twitter-trending moment for themselves. He hadn't been able to protect Maia twelve days beforehand, he could at least protect her memory from being used as a prop in someone else's story, job appraisal or merit award application.

He struggled for things to say. He made it easy for himself by selecting details, anecdotes unknown to the professionals, but not too many. Some stories would remain within the family. He threw in a few references to events that the public relations people or gate-crashers would struggle to explain should they find themselves accosted by a television camera in the next twenty-four hours. That said, he caught excerpts of statements read out by support services that were wholly irrelevant to his little friend. Who wrote them? Who approved them?

There was no representative from the zoo which was probably a good thing. If someone had turned up at the church it would have been to a chorus of boos and tutting from the gathered crowds. But he couldn't blame the zoo and keep a clear conscience himself.

In his words to the mourners he thanked the public for their support and their generosity in donating to the money-giving webpage. He thanked those who signed the book of condolence and expressed the hope that Maia would be long remembered. He thanked Maia for being Maia and he thanked her for helping him be a better person.

'A man becomes a better man by way of unclehood,' he had said, 'and by the hard and patient work of a trusting niece.'

He had planned to say more. There was another paragraph. But he had stalled. Not by grief, but, dare he admit it, anger. He couldn't utter the next words on his lips – 'you stupid, stupid little girl; you gullible, gurgle-filled piece of nonsense'. If only she had grown up more quickly and become like her siblings (in fact, like everybody else) and ignored him.

As he stood holding the paper, staring into nothingness and visualising words he could never share, a ripple of applause drifted into the church from the crowds outside until it was adopted by the seated congregation itself until pew after pew rose in applause and tears. So wrong. So very, very wrong. And all because of that stupid, stupid, little girl and her stupid, stupid lions.

Thus, for him, the televised funeral show didn't really catch the mood. Along with Maia's brothers and sisters he would pay his respects to her in a week or two, visiting the empty grave.

The watching commentators described Maia's uncle as someone no little girl should be without. And, 'remarkably for her tender age, she had known it,' they solemnly reported.

His insides sank further. He needed to talk to his sister.

– VII – Week Three, Tuesday

The Tuesday of the third week (of the four that changed his life forever) was, in the words of the press liaison person, a 'fantastic day' – 'the best yet'. A money-giving page set up by a stranger in the wake of Maia's 'murder by lion' (Gemma's words) to support Maia's mother and siblings had passed the £50,000 target in a matter of hours. After the funeral the funds had soared, many citing the halting (but brilliant) words of the uncle as a source of inspiration. It now stood at £720,000. The press liaison lady was thrilled. It was the most successful 'thing [she] had ever been involved with'. He almost wondered whether she would now make a point of searching out 'murdered' children causes and specialise in servicing the niche market (for an appropriate consultation fee) having worked the 'Maia-lion' case.

A consensus had emerged from social media and other consultation that £500,000 should be passed to the family enabling them to move to a new home and provide some holiday and educational opportunities for the other children. The mother couldn't work in the short term (three grieving children) and the father was absent. It was the community helping a community member in a time of need. Any remaining funds should be placed in a charitable trust to support a cause largely of benefit to children (and somehow related to the tragedy, perhaps).

He was happy to absent himself from the discussions and was even grateful that the matter helped keep people busy and away from the family. It was only when he learnt that discussions were moving towards the name and logo of the charity that he involved himself.

'Maia's Courage' sounded like a beer. The 'Courage of Maia' didn't sound like anything he could put his finger on, but he didn't like it. The inclusion of the name 'Maia' was not to be permitted at all, he insisted, and a reference to a lion was problematic. His sister was too weak to contest any proposed idea, but he was thinking of Gemma, Emily and Marcus. Nor should it have an image of a child either. Early drafts had included a silhouette of a child (or the close up of a child's facial feature) with a lion, but his sister and Maia's siblings kept bursting into tears when they saw the logo because it was a constant reminder of the nature of Maia's demise. There was no way that their baby sister should be forever associated with lions. So the image of a child and her name were removed altogether. 'Let's put a positive spin on things,' some young hopeful had said, 'let's include words like 'bravery, strength' – the 'Bravery of Lions' perhaps?'

He realised that it was intended to suggest that Maia had had the bravery of a lion, but the suggestion brought the most piercing squeal of all from both Gemma and Emily. It was as if they were praising the courage of the six lions for stepping up to the plate, quite literally.

He quickly realised he had a veto over the use of Maia's name, but not a reference to a lion. He grudgingly understood an oblique reference to the miserable events would ultimate help enable funds to be raised for a good cause. But what exactly was the cause? What could the charitable funds be used for?

'What would Maia want it for? Lions?' someone asked chirpily.

'An animal charity?' said another trying to fill the silence.

No. Not animals, he insisted. He didn't like the idea that the result of Maia being fed to lions helped lions be better fed. Besides, contributing to the caged-life for any living creature seemed counter to the instinct of any three year old he had met. Supporting family units who struggle. This seemed sensible. Seeing the discussion move away from Maia and lions, he relaxed and stepped back; when discussion moved to supporting the successful mentoring of young children (making them fearless, helping them confront their fears), he shrunk back.

In the vacuum created by his hesitancy, a momentum was established. All children needed an 'uncle' figure (or aunt) allowing single-parent families access to wise counsel, everyday relief from the home – a charity that supported (supervised) trips to the zoo, the seaside, art centres. A charity to relieve the everyday stress and burden on the single parent. The charity could raise a profile for the need to develop an infra-structure linking families to suitable mentors. A charity to help banish fear from children's lives. It would be the ultimate testament to Maia – she who, by being fearful, became fearless. In time, lions would be fearful, not feared.

It would all dissolve away in a few weeks or months, he thought, as he shrunk back further and exited the room.

– VIII – Week Three, Wednesday

Nearly a week had passed since the Maia's funeral. The fundraising, gift-giving element was in the final throes of organisation. His role in the palaver was at an end. He could withdraw. Now was the time for the conversation with his sister. It was Wednesday of the third week (of the four that would change his life forever).

It had seemed such a long time since they had sat together as brother and sister. And here they were. The medication was being stepped down. She was listening.

'So, as you know,' he continued, 'a couple of times a week I go to the café and have my cooked breakfast. Scrambled egg, two sausages, a fried tomato, a café latte and a pastry (usually pecan). Altogether it came to £5.20. I rarely stray from the selection, because the choice is limited. Pedro is from Spain and seems always pleased to see me and knows my order, so all is well. He puts my breakfast together, I pay him the £5.20.

'Anyway one day some weeks ago, Pedro was preparing my breakfast, but as I moved to the till with my £5.20 ready in my hand, Hazel, Pedro's manager and quite a formidable lady, was on the till helping out. She reviewed the items on my plate and tapped in the order on the till whereupon the breakfast came to £6.50. I was more than happy to pay the higher amount but I floundered around with my purse and wallet trying to find the additional coins all under her watchful eye, before handing over a ten pound note.'

His sister nodded. He could see she was being patient, but she was struggling. Beyond the thin membrane of composure, the turbulent insanity of grief swirled, he thought. He mustn't dally.

'As Hazel handed over the change to me she leaned forward and whispered, 'how much does Pedro normally charge you?''

' 'What, oh? I don't know,' I mumbled in reply.'

'It's just that I saw that you had the change ready in your hand. I just want to check,' Hazel said.'

' 'Oh, it varies, five to six pounds, but it varies,' I said, but the damage had been done. I knew what would happen. She would give Pedro a telling off for regularly undercharging me.'

'OK,' his sister said nodding and wincing. Looking at her it would be unclear whether the drugs were kicking in or fading away. He knew that his sister's daughter had been eaten by lions just two weeks earlier, but the story was important. It was relevant. She needed to know.

'I felt bad for Pedro. I went off and ate my breakfast, but five minutes later I could see her talking to him sternly while animatedly giving a demonstration of the cash till's operation. He looked beaten up. I felt terrible, but what could I do? Anyway, I left.'

'OK, oh dear,' his sister sighed, visibly relaxing, no doubt in the belief it was broadly speaking a happy ending – no one was torn to pieces by wild animals. (Or perhaps she was relieved because she thought the story was over? He couldn't tell.)

'Anyway,' he continued, 'the following week I did not know whether to go to the café and have my breakfast. What would I say to Pedro? I had got him into trouble. So I only went once the following week but at a time I knew he would not be there. But I felt bad.'

His sister nodded, a pained expression suddenly visited upon her face.

'Please help me understand why you are telling me this?' she whispered.

The question threw him off his stride. Responding to his sister would delay the crux of the story yet further. He ignored the question and persevered.

'I felt foolish being scared, but knew I could not go on like this. I needed my breakfasts. I would just have to turn up and roll my eyes and apologise for getting him into trouble. I had to step up and confront my fears.'

'Why are you telling me this?' his sister cried. 'Please. I don't care and about your cooked breakfasts. My daughter was eaten by lions and I .....'

'Because I was telling Maia the story about...'

'I don't care,' she whimpered, 'I don't care,' before collapsing back into the sofa too tired even to sob. Perhaps he shouldn't have started the conversation with the words 'it was important and it might bring closure'. He tried to take some solace in his attempt. He would leave it a few days and try telling the cooked breakfast story again. He could keep it shorter next time assuming the medication hadn't wiped her memory clean. Perhaps waiting until immediately after the funeral was still too soon. He should wait. Maybe next week. In the meantime he should get the remaining arrangements for the blasted charity business out of the way.

– IX – Week Three, Friday

It was Friday of the third week (of four that would change his life for ever). Friday was not the day for talking. It was a day for news.

The zoo and zoo-keeper had been a few of the topics of conversation during the previous few weeks. After all, questions still remained. The press had done their best to answer some of the questions (or rather persist in asking certain questions again and again).

Who was the zoo-keeper?

How could a three year old girl climb into an enclosure unnoticed?

What were the emergency procedures?

Who was on guard?

Who was responsible?

Who was responsible?

Who was responsible?

Although these questions were subsequently repeated in his sister's living room in bouts of despair and high tension, they were also being asked of the zoo. The owner had sweated through a press conference. The zoo manager had mumbled from prepared statements standing outside the gates of the zoo. Finally, the keeper of lions himself had been asked time and time again as he trudged grim-faced down a residential street only to turn through a small garden gate of a modest terraced home often bathed in the cold, harsh, lightening flashes of photographic scrutiny.

The news-giver, the press liaison lady, did not know how to break the news. Was it good news or bad? She played it safe and kept her options open. Raising her intonation towards the end of the sentence allowed her to both maintain a positive intonation (a 'result' for Team Maia) for any following sentence or adopt a tone of sadness (for any following sentence) as she dropped the intonation on the exhale. It all depended on the reaction of Maia's mother.

'The zoo-keeper has committed suicide.'

The news was met by stunned silence. Unsure whether this was agreeable news or yet more misery, the press liaison lady maintained a quiet series of shallow breaths ready to go either way.

He was almost too exhausted to react himself. God only knows what his sister must be feeling.

He looked at his sister watching the press liaison person. The grieving mother had no strength to react. Was it justice? Or did she somehow feel responsible for yet more anguish for another family? Looking back towards the press liaison lady, he saw the woman flounder in the absence of a response from his sister. Feeling pity for all concerned he rose to his feet to invite the visitor to leave the room. However, feeling she had one more ace to play, the press liaison lady stood her ground this time knowing the tone she would strike.

'On a cheerful note,' the lady said to Maia's mother, 'it has been proposed that you should be the Honorary President of the charity.'

Whereupon the bearer of 'good news' herself felt Maia's uncle consoling hand on her arm before being escorted from the room.

– X – Week Three, Saturday

The Saturday (in the third week of the four that would change his life forever) was a day that should slip into the ether, never to be heard of again. Twenty-four hours that should be dissolved in a vat of acid. One whole revolution of the planet that should be tied to a lump of concrete and dropped in the ocean. He stood in the kitchen of his sister's house at 9.30 a.m.. He was alone but for a house full of uniforms – police and paramedics. His nieces and nephews had already been ushered off the premises by neighbours. They would learn the news that afternoon. He wasn't going to tell them. It was too much. He would leave it to the professionals. He wondered whether his ex-brother-in-law would arrive. The father hadn't known Maia, but he had known Maia's mother, the mother to his three other children. A mother whose own life had now been taken.

'We can't wake her,' the neighbour had said, breathlessly when he answered the continuous knocking on his front door that morning.

He hadn't said anything as he immediately stumbled out of the house after his sister's neighbour.

'We've called an ambulance,' she panted as she tried to run the hundred yards to the sister's house. The neighbour had probably not run since school sports days, he thought. The woman's body was wholly unaccustomed to anything other than ponderous movement. As his thoughts turned to what she was saying, he thought the world was now sufficiently strange that a huge fissure would open up in front of them and into which both of them would fall, never to be found. In fact it seemed only right and just, but running another ten, twenty yards, the ground did not move. There was no sudden darkness at his feet, the concrete asphalt path underfoot remained firm. This cannot be.

He had seen the paramedics trying to revive his sister on her bed, but she looked too pale. She was gone. He saw the paramedics rifling through the bottles on her bedside table looking for clues. They were spoilt for choice. Too many combinations. There would be questions. Doctors would be embarrassed. Like her, he had to get away. He slipped away to the kitchen.

There were only two sounds that forced their way into his consciousness that morning: the continual heavy footfalls on the crushed staircase carpet and the whispered sentence: 'What those children need right now is their uncle.'

Almost immediately the very opposite sentiment ran through his own mind. In fact right now he was a danger to man, woman and child.

As the evening encroached he felt he had lost something else that day – a feeling that the horrors might be coming to an end. Besides the need to be supportive to his sister and her family, the only thing on his radar was helping her through the appearance at the upcoming press conference to announce the founding of the charity. As the night claimed the day altogether, he wondered: did this mean more or fewer press conferences?

– XI – Week Four, Tuesday

'Just how proud are you of what you have done?' was the first question of the Tuesday of the fourth week (of four that would change his life forever) at the first press conference since the passing of his sister. It caught him off-guard. He didn't reply. Fortunately another question hit him.

'How pleased are you to be the Honorary President of the charity aimed at providing wise counsel to children in need?'

Thus he found himself in front a moving black mass again. He didn't want to be there, but if he wasn't then some other press liaison person would be centre stage. Who knows, this time the press liaison person might lay claim to having known his sister, even claiming to be a friend. She or he might claim to feeling like one of the family. No, no more. It was one last painful event.

Now a seasoned professional, he had played firm and was not permitting cameras for the funeral itself, nor did he have anything to do with any impromptu press conference about his sister's demise. If he had known better (and had the time), he would have played firmer with arrangements for the charity and its launch. If Maia's mother had lived longer, it might have changed again, but everybody was tired. As the charity trustees had said, it was important that Maia's mother agree with them (not, he noted, that they should consider the ideas of a grieving mother). Hopes aside, everything was lost in the passing of Maia's mother and the subsequent funeral arrangements.

A remarkable £1.75 million had been donated by the public. No images of Maia (or his sister) were to be used in any way for the promotion of the charity's work. He was duty-bound to protect the likenesses of his sister and niece. There would be images from the press conference which would be enough. He dared not look at the final logo on the banner screen behind him. A lion is a lion is a lion. He left it to the press person to explain to the black, flashing, moving mass that no child should fear lions. All they needed was mentoring to become lions themselves. They needed wise counsel. Wise uncles.

'Do you think Maia would be proud of you and what you have achieved?' was the final question.

Just in case the uncle's pause became a little too awkward the press liaison lady leaned forward and, furrowing her brow as if it was a stupid question, replied, 'Of course, she would be proud of her uncle, of course. Who wouldn't be proud of such an uncle?'

– XII – Week Four, Sunday

On the last day of the fourth week (of the four that would change his life forever), he found himself waking in his sister's home looking at his own alarm clock. It was eight o'clock in the morning and the first day when there seemed to be no duties to perform, no arrangements to be made, no more press conferences and no more funerals. His sister's funeral had taken place on the Thursday. She was buried in the same grave as Maia. On Friday a train had overturned outside London. Many people had died. There would be lots of press conferences for the unsuspecting families. The circus had moved on. He had found himself looking to check the early reports to see if any photogenic young children had been among the fatalities. There had. In fact a school trip to a London museum had been caught up in the trauma. Life, as he had once known it, was returning to normal. Thank God.

Friends and volunteers had helpfully arranged for Gemma, Marcus and Emily to spend time with schoolfriends. It had been thought good for them to get out of the house, even spend time away from the place they had once called a happy home. They would move premises in due course, but for the time being their uncle had moved in and would be 'wise counsel to them all' or so the family liaison had told them. As he braced himself to seize another day, he heard downstairs the helpful neighbour volunteer to organise the grieving Emily's day-bag. He rose and stepped into the shower in a bathroom full of small toothbrushes and cartoon soap. It would be like this from now on, he thought. The children would not join their father in

Canada. Nobody wanted such an arrangement, so nobody would describe it as a scandal.

Arriving in the kitchen he was met with a smile and a stroke of the arm by the neighbour volunteer woman person formally appointed by someone to assist in 'the transition' (mostly his own). The children were up and organising their bags and coats without meeting the eyes of anybody else in the house. Before long there were knocks on the door, hugs, arms over shoulders as the youngsters were escorted to cars and nine hours of distraction with friends.

Then silence. The house was empty but for him and the volunteer.

He felt a hand on his arm.

'What do you normally do on a Sunday?'

'What?'

'Before all this? What would you normally do on a Sunday?' she asked softly, with a soft smile, her hand still resting softly on his forearm, her head tilted as if softly resting on a soft cushion strapped to her shoulder.

He paused and thought. It was a world away. An age. A different time. A different place.

'I'd start the day with a cooked breakfast at the Jericho café.'

'Well, there you go then, a cooked breakfast it is,' she said. 'You go. I'll tidy up here.'

Before he knew it, he was moving down Walton Street. Almost gliding. There was a slight sense of dread deep inside but he couldn't place or establish why. He entered the café. He was a changed man. He moved over to the counter and recognised the Spanish staff member. Pedro, his name was? Yes, that's right.

The café breakfast marked on the chalk board looked no different to the one buried deep in his memory.

'Er, Pedro. Hello,' he said smiling and suddenly aware he ought to refer to the under-charging embarrassment in their last meeting.

Pedro, looking startled, said nothing. What could he say in English? What could he say in Spanish? He just pursed his lips together and nodded and hoped his face would say it all. The uncle didn't know what his own face looked like. Since his last visit he had endured two deaths in the family and inherited the care of three broken little people.

With the raising of his finger towards the menu board and a twitch of his eyebrows, the breakfast order was placed. Scrambled egg on one slice of toasted granary bread, two sausages, half a fried tomato, a skinny café latte and a pecan pastry. Pedro quietly thanked his lucky stars that half the preparation of the breakfast order could be done with his back to the customer.

Suddenly aware that the longer he lingered the more awkward Pedro would feel, he started to fiddle with his wallet in readiness for payment.

'No, no, no,' said Pedro shaking his head on seeing the wallet. 'No money. On the house.'

'No, no, I will pay the £6.50. I know it has gone up. Pedro. I remember.'

'No, no,' an older man's gruff voice boomed from the back of the café.

The owner who normally grumpily hung back behind the counter sauntered forward followed by duty manager Hazel. Both joined Pedro's side.

His voice firm, 'No, not today,' the owner said waving a finger before nodding in the direction over the grieving uncle's shoulder. The uncle turned and looked. Standing large and proud in the window was a 'Fear of Lions' fundraising stand, with poster and large collection box. All in bright eye-catching lion yellow. His eyes fell upon an image of himself staring blankly out from the poster above the words:

'You too can be an uncle.'

He didn't know where the picture had been taken. Presumably the press conference? Printed below his broken features in large bold font were the words: 'No Fear, Just Wise Counsel.'

There had been talk of the charity's name. 'Fear of Lions' was sufficiently ambiguous. Maia feared lions but had confronted them. Cleverly, however, someone thought the phrase could suggest the lions feared the brave little girl (apparently nobody was in the room to speculate that the lions had successfully confronted their own fears when they launched the attack).

Lost in the moment of bright, positive, life-affirming yellow, he knew his own life had changed forever. His 'lost moment' was broken, as if by design, by the stepping forward into his line of sight of a little old lady and the slipping of her five pound note into the collection box. All of which was completed with a warm, sensitive, respectful and soft smile directed at the customer standing motionless at the till.

The ashen-faced uncle turned back towards Pedro and the café staff whereupon he noticed the Fear of Lions badges pinned to their breasts. In unison they nodded respectfully as Pedro uttered the morning's final words.

'Mr President.'

The Totty Boat

– I– Space-Time

Hey buddy,

I will write other letters about ambition, plans, friendship and adventure, but this is the one that matters. Not matters the most I think, but, like dark matter, weighs the heaviest.

You're a young man, but before you hit double figures I need to share with you some thoughts and experiences. After all, knowledge should be shared between generations. Don't listen to your mother, I'm not grumpy, I'm just knowledgeable in a man's way. You'll understand one day. (Also, important: Don't let your mother read this.)

There is no head start in life unless it addresses the topic of totty. Therefore, I hope these words will give you a helping hand, because me putting pen to paper now will allow you to consider these things in your teens, your twenties and even your thirties, after which you will no doubt be well-placed to write your own letter to your own nephew (or even son).

For millennia there has been a certain cultural expectation to find a mate for life. Arguably it is becoming more difficult now – more 'personal choice', more (or less) societal and familial pressure, longer life-spans et cetera. They all complicate matters. However, I will keep it simple, even scientific. I think I can summarise it in terms of physics (space-time). In short, a person should form a romantic relationship based not on whom you want to be with, but the person *you* want to be. It requires careful consideration and choice of mate, in other words (and to be frank), not any old totty will do. There are different types. So, in order to choose wisely, you should first understand the totty-types to which you are drawn, those types for which you have a weakness.

Here is the nub: it is not about the lady herself. It is about the feeling the lady induces in you; the place she takes you. In my youth I could not read the feelings, but eventually life brought me to a point where I only responded to a handful of lady-induced feelings. The challenge has been which one of the short-listed lady-feelings I truly hanker after (or is it 'after which I hank'?).

This is where bringing physics into this discussion helps. Therefore, like Einstein, I will articulate these matters with regard to 'space' and 'time'. Who knows, maybe if he had lived longer (or lived bolder) he might have tried to write something on this topic himself. Alas no, it has fallen to your uncle to elucidate on space invaders and beach time. (By 'space', I mean both the literal 'physical space' and 'head-space'.)

In my few decades of lady-play there have been a handful of space-invaders who took up more space than others and I have now been able to identify the five types. The question has been which of these five types were contenders for, dare I say, 'space travel'. I spent many years unable to decide between these totty types, but after a prolonged period of reflection and experimentation, I have finally identified the one type most suitable for me.

Remember, strictly speaking these space-invader-totty-types are the 'induced-lady-feelings' and not the ladies themselves. (To try and categorise ladies directly is far too difficult even for a scientist.) My types are: the car workshop; the silk dress; the satin sheets; the orange grove and, finally, the forest stream. These five types are peculiar to me. Your induced-lady-feelings ('totty-types') will take you to different places and you will give them different names. I do not pretend to be able to give you advice on what type will be right for you, but those described below should act as an example.

– II – Space (Totty-types)

My first type is the car workshop or, more accurately, the garaged classic car (a type afflicted on most men). The vehicle itself is a perfectly engineered piece of machinery that looks and moves as if it were tooled by gods. It is unearthly both in design and engineering. People sigh as the marvel glides past on the streets. However, I place the classic car in a mechanic's workshop under a railway bridge arch in a forgotten part of town. The treasure lifts, even overwhelms, its surroundings yet remains very much part of it. The wondrous feat of engineering gleams amidst its grimy world of dust and oil.

The car is carefully maintained by a mechanic (you, me) – a gifted craftsman who knows and loves motor-craft. Even to him the sight of the machine inspires a sense of wonder. It demands attention. How could such an object of beauty exist in such a dank and dreary world? Its environment stands in such unrelenting starkness to the invention and beauty of the engineering. One cannot but admire the lines, the design, power, the craftsmanship and the object itself.

But that is the problem with this totty-type. Firstly, one is almost overwhelmed by admiration. It is just too splendid, too serene a creation. Secondly, there is a nagging sense that the 'inspiration of awe' is in some way its prime function. As the years have passed I have come to ask myself a question: do I want to spend my time in a garage marvelling at a beautiful piece of machinery that overwhelms its surroundings? Somewhat reluctantly, I came to the conclusion that I did not. Nay, could not.

My second category is the black silk dress. On meeting the type, one is conflicted. The heat generated by the thought of acquaintance with the lady is simultaneously cooled by her soothing presence. As a fabric, silk both excites and cools in the heat of the desert while its black colour is neutral but striking. The dress gives nothing away and makes no statement of intent. You almost feel that you become one with the dress falling over her lines and clinging to her figure as she moves and breathes, soaking up the perfume secreted from the soft pores of the hidden flesh. Whilst clinging to the curves of the soft skin, one is pulled and stretched as limbs move and chest heaves. Yet, one is ultimately haunted by the thought – do I want the drama of being a dress? Is that my star trek? From dust to fabric to dust? Material cut to size only to fall over the shape of another? At my age I am too old to be cut to, and be defined by, another's shape. However delightful that shape might be.

Totty-type three: the satin sheets. Similar to type two, but different enough to have its own category. This lady makes you feel like you are lying and twisting on a bed of satin sheets. Soft and luxurious, it is a restful place from which one never wants to move. After all, why would one want to move from such luxury, such softness? Surely it is the perfect state? One is not surrounded by the grime of a garage nor defined by the shape and lines of another. Yet, however comfortable you feel, there is, deep inside, the knowledge that from the bed you must rise. You know that your journey between the stars isn't all about comfort, being curled up in a ball of peace and grace. There is an ache for exploration, for drama, and it will never be found in the swirling luxury of satin sheets. One must feel the sun and rain on the face, one's back and limbs as one strains and aches with effort. It is with regret that one cannot sustain a fulfilling life in the luxury of satin. Such luxury is not for the young man and not for a lifetime. When one is old and tired, then perhaps satin sheets are coveted, but they are hardly required. This third totty-type, however tempting, is not right for a young man. One must rise from the bed and venture out.

Totty-type quattro. The fourth category of lady is indeed blessed with the warmth of the sun. She is the orange grove. What more could one want than the company of fresh nutritious fruit? Peel past the protective layer to expose the soft succulent, nourishing insides. To lie in a grove dedicated to the production of such natural delights is heavenly. Oranges should be a daily part of a healthy diet. With this kind of lady I have been nourished to full health in the blessed warmth of a secure and dedicated environment. But again, where is the balance? Can there be too much of a good thing? Where is the beer? The meat? The chocolate brownie? I could not dispute that being in the presence of this kind of woman would be an agreeable way to live. Such a person could not be the cause for any complaint, but sadly, an orange grove is built with one fruit in mind. One plan. Good health needs balance. Where is the shade from the blazing sun? Groves are artificial constructs and tend to be walled or fenced to keep out the world. It could be fear, melancholy or a life not lived. To live one's life on an endless supply of good fruit misses an element of 'journey'. One can value orange groves and everything associated with them, but one cannot make one's life with (and within) an orange grove. No.

Finally, there is the forest stream. Or the woman who takes you to the floor of the forest where you lie, with eyes half-closed. The heat and brightness of the sun hanging in the blue sky is softened by the canopy of trees gently swaying in the breeze above you. The heat of the day invisibly permeates the forest, but you are comfortable because you are lying in the shallowest of forest streams. Water splashes over your scalp cooling and slowing your busy brain. It runs down from your neck finding new ways down your spine cooling the heat of the outside world, nature's very own caress pinching you alert to the peace. You are alone in a forest full of life resting for a moment in an environment that has existed for an age. From this soil you have risen and to this cool earth you shall return, until you are called to the stars, as dust.

The forest stream is nature's fabric. It soothes, cools yet stimulates the senses. There are no walls, fences, doors, beds, man-made fabric. Your peace is guarded by the majesty of the forest. The fauna hides you, the trees stand guard. You are soothed and fed by the coolness of the stream. This is the lady-feeling I want – the forest stream.

Your totty-types will be different. You might find solace in the grime and oil of a garage or meaning in a fabric or destiny in a grove. Or others lost to me. It is your space, nobody else's.

– III – Time (The Beach, the Ocean, the Boat)

Then there is the beach of life that stretches out as far as you can see. It is as long as your longest walk and it holds all time. A wide and sandy playground. The warm sand melts between your toes and around your feet as you run, walk, dance and play. You may never want to leave. After all, why would anyone want to be anywhere else? Regardless of the number of passing beachfarers the space is open, eternal. Yet if it proves too noisy, then off among the dunes you can slink and find solitude.

The beach's partner is, of course, the ocean. An ocean of time forever lapping upon the shore. Boats gently bob in the shallows, all the while being softly tugged out to sea. Does one succumb to the whisperings of the ocean, climb aboard a boat and venture out on to the sea?

There was a time when totty would pass me on the beach. A flicker in their countenance would acknowledge my passing, but this fades in time and soon most beachfarers look straight through you. There is no flicker of recognition. One becomes beach furniture around which others manoeuvre, their eyes set on the horizon or something further down the beach. You begin to feel like the flotsam and jetsam you've been stepping over all your life.

This is how it happens. And when it does, it is too late.

If you are not careful you will find yourself arriving breathless at an embarkation point only to learn that the totty boat has sailed. The totty with whom you might have journeyed the oceans, trekked between the stars, have themselves boarded a vessel and, their eyes fixed on the open ocean ahead of them, drifted away out to sea leaving you alone on the shore to be mocked by the ocean's waves. Nobody tells you the totty boat will sail. You might think there will be another schooner along in a minute. You might see boats ready for departure in the distance, but they are moored at the base of a rainbow. You don't qualify for ocean passage and you cannot follow. You might see others attempt to swim out to the departing craft, but they are only destined to be smashed on the rocks and swept back to shore as unrecognizable driftwood.

Before long you'll turn to survey the beach, but however far you walk all you will pass is seashore paraphernalia. You'll meander along the sand slowly adjusting to life without ocean passage. Beach furniture might invite you to sit and share. Flotsam quietly rots. Beached whales cry. Blubbery seals honk. Waddling penguins, crabs and all manner of wildlife, pass by. Finally, you'll look out to the sea's distant unbroken blue horizon and know nothing is out there; no boat will come. Ocean passage is about departure, not arrival.

In youth the beach heaves with traffic and some folk jostle for space on the myriad of boats. Arguably, there is no rush, after all there are so many. Besides there are games of volleyball, beachball and throw-and-catch to distract you, but don't get caught up in the games for too long. Should you come across a totty-type with whom you find yourself in step, take note. It does not necessarily mean you will always share the same length of stride, but there is a chance that by walking the sand together the two strides become one. Then, put aside the games and get busy with departure. Ball games are for the beach not the open sea.

So, good luck, buddy. Boats weren't built to stay in harbour. The only game in town is sailing. Establish your totty-types and know this, the totty boat will sail. Or, if you're not careful, you'll learn that life's just a beach and then you die.

Your doting uncle.

Acknowledgements

Many people including Danny and Arthur and family, PJB for reading, Grace Fussell for cover design, Sonja N. for artwork, David for photography. *Book of Berossus* extract translated by the author.

About the Author

Born in the UK, David O. Zeus was tutored at the Old Granville House School before having a short spell at University, after which he joined the army (11th Hussars) where he saw action at the Battle of the Hornburg. While recuperating from his injuries on the remote island of Nomanisan he began writing. He is married to Donna Mullenger and lives for most of the year in the place of his birth, Little Hintock.

www.davidozeus.uk

Upcoming Titles

Collected Stories – Volume II
Collected Stories – Volume III
Nigel (trilogy)

Printed in Great Britain
by Amazon